The Region of Lost Names

Camino del Sol

A Latina and Latino Literary Series

The Region of Lost Names

of Lost Names

A Novel

Fred Arroyo

The University of Arizona Press
Tucson

The University of Arizona Press
© 2008 Fred Arroyo
All rights reserved

Library of Congress Cataloging-in-Publication Data
Arroyo, Fred, 1966–
The region of lost names : a novel / Fred Arroyo.
p. cm. – (Camino del sol : a Latina and Latino
literary series)
ISBN-13: 978-0-8165-2657-4 (pbk. : alk. paper)
1. Loss (Psychology)—Fiction. 2. Memory—Fiction.
3. Psychological fiction. I. Title.
PS3601.R725R45 2008
813'.6—dc22   2007029696

Publication of this book is made possible in part by the proceeds
of a permanent endowment created with the assistance of a
Challenge Grant from the National Endowment for the
Humanities, a federal agency.

Manufactured in the United States of America
on acid-free, archival-quality paper.

13   12   11   10   09   08   6   5   4   3   2   1

For Jill

Who offered me the memories to dream

And for all those who came before

From far and wide

Whose dreams are colored by

Their exiled memories

And for Charles Francis Arroyo

Who may one day dream the locks

That no longer need keys

contents

I've decided to make up my mind
about nothing, to assume the water mask,
to finish my life disguised as a creek,
an eddy, joining at night the full,
sweet flow, to absorb the sky,
to swallow the heat and cold, the moon
and the stars, to swallow myself
in ceaseless flow.

—Jim Harrison, "Cabin Poem"

Part One

Ernest

For four nights Boogaloo's face appeared on the evening news: a brief, black-and-white head shot, his smiling dark face seeming much younger than the age suggested by his graying temples. There was a white cloth wrapped around his neck and, in a very peculiar way, almost like a bad joke, the cloth accentuated his peaceful smile. For four nights, Boogaloo's angelic smile, and underneath it a phone number and a few undistinguishable characteristics: middle aged, African or Hispanic American, five foot eight, thin, 140 to 155 pounds. He had no identification. The authorities needed help. But no one could identify him; Boogaloo was the only name he gave.

I never witnessed any of these reports, and perhaps I only learned of Boogaloo's death by chance. Around 8:25, on a Monday morning, I was my punctual Monday-morning self: an hour of coffee at La Habana. A double Cubano sat on the table to my right, on my left a frangipani, and in between them I immediately recognized Boogaloo's face on the front page of the paper that someone had left behind (and with sudden composure I acknowledged gestures and sounds, smells and tastes, muscles and sweat: working with Boogaloo and my father in the fields of southwestern lower Michigan). My father would soon turn fifty-nine. Boogaloo must've only been around fifty-seven or fifty-eight. I read the caption underneath the photograph and then turned back to page twelve, where Boogaloo's story continued.

He had attended an AA meeting. He sat in the back of the room, his hands folded on his lap, a witness recalled, and he was conscientiously immersed in the evening's testimonies. He wore a black suit, his salt-and-pepper hair swept back off his forehead with pomade; his hands were unmistakable, the witness remembered, wrinkled and work worn, and half of his right pinkie was missing. Boogaloo stood up, smoothed down his beautiful silver tie, and gave a moving testimony of his life after drinking, his current life as a cook. His only regret was not being a part of his daughter's life, and he wondered if his years of drinking had ruined his chances of ever knowing her. He briefly commended everyone present for sharing their stories and finished with an eloquent plea: *Remember that the dream of one is the dream of everyone*. The group broke out in applause.

When the meeting ended, a man approached and thanked Boogaloo for his encouraging words. They shook hands, spoke briefly. Boogaloo turned to leave, and just before he reached the back exit of the YMCA he collapsed. Shortly thereafter he died of a cerebral hemorrhage.

I looked up from the paper. Without even thinking—for a moment the memory of sharp silver flashed through my mind, and the rough nub of Boogaloo's pinkie—I folded the paper in half and dropped it into the empty chair to my right. A pool of morning sunlight gleamed on the marble tabletop, the coffee cup bright and clean.

I received the news about Boogaloo too late. The night before he had been cremated, and on the very next day his ashes would be disposed of, the paper flatly stated. A leaf skidded across the sidewalk; I saw a white cloth flapping on a clothesline, imagined ashes swirling in the wind, falling into the sea.

I picked up my coffee, looked into the deep brown black, and thought of my father: if he lived here, he would not only identify Boogaloo but he would probably take him back to Puerto Rico. I felt then, as I swallowed the rest of my coffee, that I must go and identify Boogaloo. Even though I had hated Boogaloo, for he had created so much fear and shame for me when I was young, I had to go.

When I was fifteen, I worked in the fields alongside men who had worked there since they had been children, men who seemed to walk with a stoop straight toward death. Boogaloo's smile; his face, broad and black; his teeth, white and straight; his mouth mocking me, calling me hijo.

Hurry up, hijo . . .

You are falling behind, hijo . . .

4

I don't know what's worse, hijo, you or the viejo . . .

These men and Boogaloo didn't seem to feel any pain, they just worked as long as the smiles, jokes, and laughter lasted, as long as they could sing loud and move faster and faster down the endless rows of corn.

> Que me duele la cabeza
> Tráme una cerveza
> Que me duele el corazón
> Tráme un palo de ron

The melody rose up in me, pulsing like a deep stream running through my biceps, and I knew I had to go. It was the least I could do. I won't take him back to Puerto Rico, I thought, I can't do that; but I should, at the very least, send him to my father. I must do so; Boogaloo had helped me bring my father home so many times before.

I picked up the cup and saucer. A shaft of light caught my eyes—I squinted, the cup and saucer trembling, the sound too high, hollow, empty. I set them back on the table. I closed my eyes for a moment, listened to the jingling bell on the door, a long, dark row leading through a field.

Earlier this spring, near the end of March, I stepped into a café. There was a demitasse filled with coffee, a twisting trail of steam rising above the rim. The sunlight inside the café, luxurious and welcomed, brushed away the hard wind on the bluff. I turned from the counter with my cup of coffee. Sitting at a bistro table near the window, drinking espresso and reading the paper, was a thin, elegantly dressed man. He wore a long-sleeved guayabera of lime green, freshly pressed black slacks, and around his neck, a lovely purple scarf. I paused, stilled with recognition—*Boogaloo.*

He called out my name, Ernest, *Ernestito,* and abruptly stood up. We hugged, his scarf soft against my neck. I felt Boogaloo's ribs and his hips; yet my sudden concern disappeared because Boogaloo seemed so happy and well, though much older than the last time I had seen him (it had been fifteen or sixteen years, and I never imagined he still lived in Michigan).

We stood back. Looked at each other. We held hands; Boogaloo tightly gripping my hands and lightly swinging them in the air between us. He let go, and instinctively we shook the solidarity way.

It is good to see you, Ernestito. Please, come sit, Boogaloo suggested, gesturing to the chair across from him.

Good to see you, too, Boogaloo, I said, still a little stunned, and for a moment filled with angst wondering how good it was to actually see him

5

once again. When my parents left for Puerto Rico there was nothing left for me around Niles—I was all alone. I escaped to South Bend, and then to Chicago; Niles was the hometown I was always leaving, though it never let me get away. Whenever I came through this part of Michigan on my way north, I couldn't get through it fast enough. If I stopped anywhere, like on this day for coffee, I walked with my head down, trying my best not to remember or be remembered.

I didn't know, I said; well, I imagined you had moved back to Puerto Rico.

I sat down.

Boogaloo took a small sip from his espresso.

No, no. I've been all around. South Bend for a bit, Gary for a while, and then in Chicago for many years. Working, you know, factories, cooking . . . Marshall Fields for a time, in the Walnut Room. And now here in Michigan again, just north out of town.

I looked over the neatness of his clothes, the tightness of his flesh against his cheekbones, the clarity and intensity of his eyes: he looked wonderful, smiling broadly with his still-bright white teeth, and I waited, expecting some harsh, mean words from the only Boogaloo I knew.

He smiled, cleared his throat.

I remembered my father, at a much younger age, standing next to me on the parapet of El Morro, his arm around my waist, his warm hip, both of us looking out onto the caracoling sea, the smell of almonds, and then the sea breeze deafening my ears, blowing smoothly through my hair.

You look good, Boogaloo, really good, in fact.

Thank you. I'm okay, sober for a long time, and I like my life. He raised his cup to his lips but then set it back down.

But you, Ernestito, you are doing well—heading north, no? Near Traverse City?

Yes, but how . . . ?

Oh, everyone is proud of you. Your mother and father, and Magdalene, too. They're all happy.

Boogaloo shrugged, sliced the air with his open flat hand.

I talk to your father from time to time.

I turned toward the window, the cobblestones of the street blue in the midday sun. Magdalene, I thought—she must have told my parents I'm working up north.

Your dream, Ernestito, has become everyone's dream. I mean, everyone sees the choices you've made, the life you live. They miss you, of course, but they think you are happy, have become who you want to be. They respect that.

Boogaloo waved his forefinger in the air with that last part: *They respect that*.

Unsure of what to do or say on that day, I looked around the room, avoiding Boogaloo's eyes. Here we were, like two ghosts, I thought, who had become new, living beings, sitting at a small bistro table surrounded by the sound of Mozart, the smell of coffee and chocolate, thick green plants growing profusely in the strong light falling through the front windows. Behind Boogaloo's head, on the wall, there was a watercolor of a small fishing boat struggling amid white waves, a lone lighthouse throwing a beam of light on the sea, trying to guide the boat home.

They think you are happy . . .

After my parents left for Puerto Rico and I went out on my own, I never believed I'd meet Boogaloo again. I had always recognized that there would be consequences for living my life around men like Boogaloo: *they are a deep source of loneliness, despair, and work, whom I accept, no matter how easy my life has become*. At times, over the years, however, I thought I would never fully let them enter into the dream of my being. That I could keep Boogaloo in the shadowy periphery—*walking up a dusty lane, stooping in a row of corn, throwing bags of potatoes, opening a door to a bar*—and from the margins of my memory they could help me to shape my own sense of solitude and work, a kind of willed, self-imposed exile that, in a strange yet liberating way, would help me leave my past behind.

Boogaloo, what he had meant to me, I never cared to know, since I had only wished to banish him forever into a region of lost names.

Boogaloo slowly moved his hand across the table. His fingers warm and dry, distant and familiar, unmistakably filled with affection.

Don't worry. They understand, he told me.

He squeezed my wrist.

I hadn't talked to my parents . . . I couldn't even remember in how long. The years unfolded in front of me, a small breeze parting a field of tall grass, as I stepped ahead and listened to a quiet voice telling me each step I take is without consequence or regret. Fourteen or fifteen years had passed without our talking.

They know things you never have to say, he said.

Boogaloo's eyes were hard, almost black with the stare he gave me, and I looked deep into his face and discovered a new consequence: *Boogaloo is and will always be a part of my life, and perhaps he had never intended for me to hate.*

His lips turned into an upside-down smile, his cheekbones rising high, and his eyes lighting with wonder. He said, You are going north now, no?

I nodded.

Let us go, then, you and I. I want to show you something, before you leave.

Boogaloo held up his hands. Is that okay? Do you have the time?

Outside the café, the cool, stiff wind on my face; I let it fill my eyes, my nose, my ears, and I knew all I had was time. I bent over and stretched my legs, let the blood rush to my head, stood up, and looked out toward the freshwater sea; and for a brief moment, without shame or fear, I had the feeling that there was a chance of life; and as I took that blue sea within me, my chest filled with a tender, poignant, barely audible music: *here's a rhythm that can help me live.*

Three stick figures down below the bluff Boogaloo and I stood on ran across the sand, a rush of azure waves highlighting their path, a white string seemingly connecting them, and up above this connected trio a bright red kite shuddered, briefly glided, then took to the wind in an astonishingly graceful arc that cut through the forceful currents in the sky. The frame of the kite pushed through the red cloth, my spine bracing the wind, my heart beating within.

Only thirty-two, my life seemed fated to loneliness, perhaps an early death. Two of my best friends—Lorime, Juan—were gone. One day, as he stood on the bridge, a car stopped alongside Lorime. Four young men got out of their car, yelling and shoving and hitting him. He was beaten badly, knocked against the iron rails of the bridge, and then thrown in the grass, bloodied and unconscious. He died that same evening of internal bleeding. The young men who beat him never called him by his name; *greaser, mushroom licker, queer, porto* may have been the last words Lorime had heard. Juan had drowned in the river. No one ever knew for certain how he had ended up in the paper mill's spillway, and it took some time to identify him, his face battered, bloated, and broken from striking against the logs. A fleeting, vague feeling: in my shy, perhaps quiet, austere character, I see reflected in others how they see me and what they must wonder. *When will your day come, Ernest . . . Ernestito . . . Ernesto . . . ?*

8

How can you want me? Can you ever love anyone?

Magdalene—my best friend—I avoided her questions, and she, too, had left: she left for Puerto Rico with her daughter, Isabel. I could only walk an uncharted journey; I wandered, hoping for some compass in my life, some cloud or island of grace. I had made decisions that set in motion a long journey away from the boy who had once worked in the fields, the young man who had lost his closest friends, who avoided his mother and father simply because I couldn't come to terms with the fact that throughout my childhood we had lived an impoverished, sad life defined by my father's working, drinking, and anger; and yet somehow my parents found a way to love each other once again.

I thought there was only one way to go on: to dream a life—to live in a dream—where I moved, unburdened, out into my corner of the world.

Boogaloo put his arm around my shoulder. The early spring wind of that day blew through my hair. I held him around the waist. We looked out toward the blue—blue sky, blue harbor, blue sea—and I felt Boogaloo's calm strength. The kite rose, dipped, rose. The wind roared, quieted, then filled with the sound of crashing waves. Down below, I had once gone swimming with Lorime and Juan; had gone fishing with Magdalene on the pier, and she and I had lain out on the sand under the late summer sun after swimming in the chilly sea. The circular ruins of a skating rink were visible on the edge of the beach. Men, like my father and Boogaloo, who had worked in the area used to come here on Saturday nights. The lights of the Ferris wheel spinning colors above them, the laughter of young women circling the rink, their poplin skirts billowing above their white socks, their skates, a wave of shadow and light shimmering on the parquet floor. The sounds of these blue waves. *My father met my mother down there, listening to those same waves.*

You know, Ernestito, I remember when Changó met your mother.

Boogaloo squeezed my shoulder, pointed down to the beach.

We used to work at Green Giant and came here on the weekends.

Boogaloo and I turned away and walked to his car, an old Honda Civic, the backseat filled with books and newspapers, coffee cups littering the floors.

I told him, Let's go, Boogaloo, you and I, like we're going home. I have plenty of time.

The Monday-morning sun had now moved slightly, my coffee cup half in light, half in shadow. Outside La Habana, a seagull slowly swerved and descended onto the sidewalk, picking up a small piece of bread. The tulip tree swayed in the breeze, its red and white flowers shuddering softly. What was Boogaloo doing up here in Traverse City I wondered? What was he doing here, so far north, here in a town where no one—except me—knew his name? Maybe he had come to find me. The seagull turned its head suddenly, as if it heard something, then quickly lifted from the sidewalk and flew into and beyond the pinkish red, blooming tree. The bell to the café door jingled as I reached out, catching the handle before it made its return arc, the door pushing me forward as it closed, the handle leaving a warm, firm impression in my hand; and I went out to find Boogaloo, to claim his ashes before he was thrown away.

Within a grove of birch trees there was a small tin table and two folding chairs. Boogaloo set down two plates of yuca with mojo and slices of roast pork. On my plate Boogaloo had added a piece of the crispy, reddish brown skin. We sat in this grove of trees looking out on Lake Michigan, caught up in the peace, the quiet found in the sound of the warm wind, the rustling leaves, the waves. We drank mango nectar.

After we had left the café in St. Joe I followed Boogaloo out to this small lakefront cottage. The cottage was of whitewashed brick, the windows trimmed in Caribbean blue, and stenciled in red and green above the doorway, the word *Sauce*. Boogaloo told me that they served a kind of fusion between West Indian and Mexican food, and it was often amazing how busy they were on Friday and Saturday nights; he had heard of people driving down from as far as Holland or Grand Rapids. There was a small stone-and-wood addition built onto the back, and Boogaloo led me inside.

Most of the kitchen was taken up by a thick butcher-block table, oily and rich with color—saffron, oregano, cilantro, and olive oil stained into the wood. Around the table there was a stone oven, a stove with six burners and a flat grill, and a revolving oven for slow-roasting chickens and pork. Five pots, blackened and crusty, were stacked on top of the block table, though when Boogaloo walked by and knocked one with his knuckle and

11

laughed, the pots came alive: I heard and saw the same pots my abuela cooked with in her little house in Puerto Rico.

The tender pork roasted in that kitchen now melted in my mouth. The pepper and garlic caused my tongue to tingle, the olive oil fruity in my throat.

I don't know how much you know, Ernest, but Changó is very sick, Boogaloo said.

Waves crashed in front of us, behind Boogaloo's words. The wind was strong but we were warm in that grove of trees. Then the wind stopped for a moment, the leaves slowly becoming silent. Boogaloo took a bite of yuca, his lips glistening with mojo. He raised his white napkin to his chin, wiping away sauce.

He has a disease in his eyes, a kind of malaria. When we were young, working hard during a rainy season filled with cold, I remember your father got sick, sick for weeks. Some thought he would die; I saw some people from the Red Cross on the road one day and I asked for their help. They took him to an army hospital, and he was gone for a good month. Ay, but the sickness is back, now in his eyes.

I thought of my father and tried to see him in my mind. I stared into Boogaloo's eyes, gauged whether or not he was asking anything of me. I set my plate on the table.

How long? When did he . . .?

Three months ago, maybe—I don't know. They gave him medicine for a time, then some drops, bandaged his eyes.

My father: sitting under a mango tree, a strip of gauze wrapped around his head, the outline of his eyes filled with thick, bulky cotton, his hair elegantly swept off his forehead.

I only tell you, Ernestito, because I see you.

I nodded. Looked down at the table.

Thank you; no worry, Boogaloo.

I took a bite of the crunchy skin, listened to my teeth crushing and chewing. My stomach filled with anxiousness, my hands began to tremble.

I hadn't seen Changó in fifteen years. Many years would pass, he would get older and change: his hair white, his eyes droopy and red, his hands crooked as broken, wind-gnarled trees. I would still recognize my father—anytime, anywhere—yet I felt this deep awareness that my father would not know *me*. And maybe that was what I had wanted all these years when I never took the time to stay in touch.

I talked to your father not too long ago, Boogaloo said. He sounded happy, laughing, and he was glad to have Magdalene and Isabel there.

We both set our plates down. I took a long drink.

Changó was not only the way you remember him, Ernestito. Boogaloo wiped his mouth, cleared his throat. He looked out to the lake, smiled, suddenly within some story I wanted to be a part of.

We worked—and it was hard work. We were maybe eight or nine, out in the fields, for ten or twelve hours. And there were not many boys. Changó worked with the best of the men . . .

Boogaloo paused, rubbed his right knee, and looked up into the sky, searching.

But let me say something: I want to say how good he is, how he helped many of us to keep working, and to work hard so the men wouldn't be angry with us. I remember he went away to the mainland, and one day I received a letter from some Carmen Martinez, waitress, Red Coach Grill. Your father worked there as a dishwasher, and he asked this Carmen to write me a letter. He included fifty dollars and asked me to come to the mainland.

Boogaloo fingered the purple scarf at his neck.

I was only sixteen or seventeen, what did I know? I went and bought a new shirt, and then I got drunk that night, fall-down-in-the-field drunk.

Boogaloo stopped himself, smiled, perhaps lost in that night for a moment.

It was a few years before I finally came to the mainland, and never once did Changó ask me about the money. Boogaloo laughed, briefly, his mouth turning to a frown.

I shook my head. It had been Boogaloo, some eighteen years ago, who drove me away from the fields and dropped me off in South Bend. My mother had moved there, after she had left my father, and was working downtown and living in this charming brownstone apartment. There was a wide courtyard breaking off into three different tiled sidewalks that led to tall glass-and-wood doors, and in the middle of the courtyard there was a small fountain quietly splashing and filled with the late August sun.

I must help your father, Ernest; he needs help with his pain, Boogaloo said when he dropped me off, pointing toward the dark backseat of the car. Boogaloo tucked a thick fold of money into the little pocket of my T-shirt and then patted me on the shoulder. He turned to his car, got inside, and then drove away, their friend Tino waving good-bye, my father passed out in the back seat. They were going back to the fields, would work and sober up, and then . . . and then, for a moment, I didn't care, I had a feeling it was no longer my responsibility to try and help my father escape his desperate sorrow.

I took a step into the courtyard, holding a small plastic bag with my possessions. The courtyard was cool, a slight breeze shaking the two pine trees shading the entrance, the splashing fountain gently wetting my arms. Up above, white curtains billowed inside the windows; I traced different forms behind their delicate curves, searching for my mother's figure. I stopped, suddenly afraid, ashamed, and unsure of what she might think of me, if she might look at me and only remember the day I stayed behind with my father. I turned away, walked downtown, and then took a bus to Notre Dame. The bus stopped in front of a stone building, and when I stepped off a young man came out of the building, a book open in one hand and held close to his face, a plastic bag in his other hand. He turned in front of me, said *excuse me*, his plastic bag bumping into my own. I walked forward, stepped through the door of the stone building. My eyes strained in the interior light; I blinked several times. I walked forward and got a Coke from a cooler. On my way to the cash register I found myself stopping in front of a display of books. I folded open the covers, touching the soft creamy pages, feeling the black print. The words *Jane Eyre* jumped out at me—I recalled a shaking tree, gold leaves splattered against glass, the warm, sweet smell of coffee, my mother's hand turning a page—and I picked up the book and paid for it along with the Coke. Outside the sun was warm. I took a seat on a small wooden bench under a tree, took a drink from my Coke, and began reading. I hadn't held a book in my hands for over a year. I read one paragraph, then another, underlining certain words with my index finger, saying other words over and over. All at once I felt calm, filled with a music that would never leave me alone.

I decided I would make my way back to Niles, the only hometown I had ever really known.

When I left Notre Dame it took an hour of steady walking down U.S. 31—my little plastic bag tied to my belt, my book in my hand—to make it to the state line. A couple of guys on their way to Warren Dunes gave me a ride to Niles, dropping me off on Parkway Avenue, up on the hill above my maternal grandfather's cabin on the river. I walked down the trail from the hill toward the river, and then I began my life of erasing memories: I would turn away from everyone from my past to become the young man who caught the spawning salmon that returned upriver every year; and when I sold them I would have plenty of money to drink and forget and discover a sudden, beautiful region, where I left my body to become a man no one had ever known.

Boogaloo cleared his throat. I'm sorry about Juan's death. He folded his hands in his lap. I couldn't go to the funeral. My life changed, and I didn't want to be there around those feelings . . . around . . .

I lowered my head, nodded slightly. Once, my father had talked of the lonely pain he awoke with in New York, his hands still feeling hot and red and wet from washing dishes the night before. He would go to the kiosk on the corner every morning, and they knew what he wanted, what he could afford, and they laughed in a good way, not at Changó's expense. Ah, blueberry muffin and coffee? Changó would nod, sometimes laugh, too, sliding thirty-five cents across the counter.

Once, when we were walking in a field behind a potato picker, bending and tossing loose potatoes onto a wagon moving alongside us, our arms and hair golden with sweat and dust, all of us hungover and tired, Boogaloo stopped, pulled his arm back, and threw a potato as far as our eyes could see. His lips were quivering, and then he bent over and his shoulders violently shook as he gagged with dry heaves. He straightened, pulled his shoulders back, gave us a wry little smile as he wiped his hands on the front of his pants, and he told everyone how he wasn't going to work in a field ever again. He came to the mainland to have fun, eat good, live each day smooth and light. *Suave*, he said. Be so rich I wipe my ass with one-dollar bills.

My father's voice wasn't angry and it wasn't drunk. He seemed to speak to the sky, out into the fields. He said that when his father made him quit school to work, he thought he'd never leave the fields of Puerto Rico to end up in another field. He looked at Boogaloo and reminded him of the mill on the edge of the cane field back home. Chained to the mill, always walking in a circle, was a huge white ox. That ox had walked so much that rain filled its path, the water lapping against the bottom of his stomach. My father and the other boys never spoke of the tiredness they saw in the ox's eyes. They just kept working, their burning arms unloading the carts stacked with cane. One night, in front of the fire, under a mango tree, amid all the noises of the jungle and the talking men, Changó, my father, just a young boy, composed the guaracha "The Dance of the Tired Ox."

15

That song must've kept them moving, kept them alive. They lost the pain of their skins, the longing for their families, inside that song.

Changó looked at Boogaloo again, his eyes still and deep, his hand clenched in a fist and raised in the air and swaying back and forth beside his head to the rhythm of his words: *Nine years old, nine years old, and I had dreams. Days have passed, years. When I sleep, I dream these fields.*

Changó must've always felt he was beginning alone. Maybe we must all begin alone, I thought. *There is something lonely about this life.* But he had made up that song, and I imagined all those boys, and even the men, sitting underneath that tree, and, like the coquís singing in the night, they all felt a part of that song.

Earlier in the evening, closer to the lake, just on the other side of the circle of trees Boogaloo and I sat amidst, I had walked over and looked into Boogaloo's small overnight cabin while he prepared our plates. Inside, a twin bed, a small round table, and, set into the wall, a Coleman heater. There was an electric coffeepot on the table, an ashtray, and a box of matches. Two suitcases were stacked on the seat of a chair, the top one open and filled with white, blue, and black—Boogaloo's undershirts, boxers, and socks. A rope had been strung by nails across the back wall; a few shirts and pants hung from hangers, the room brightened by the clean, pressed white chef's coat hanging from the rope. I stood on the front porch, holding the railing. Old rum bottles hung from white strings attached to the roof. I pulled a bottle close, saw the amber liquid specked with pepper and salt, garlic cloves smooth at the bottom of the bottle, little red and green peppers floating in sun-warmed pineapple juice. When Boogaloo came out of the kitchen carrying our dinner, he told me the cabin was comfortable, warm in the winter and in the summer the breeze off the lake kept it cool, the waves helping him to sleep. I heard the rest of the world falling away with the sound of water, the leaves shaking on the trees, grains of sand striking the screen in his window.

Boogaloo told me to untie a bottle and take it home.

There *is* something lonely about this life. And yet . . . and yet . . . Boogaloo's life seemed complete; and perhaps so because Boogaloo had come so far, because he had taken hold of his own corner of the world, no matter how limited, impoverished, or lonely it appeared.

I took a sip of the mango nectar, watching Boogaloo's strong scarred fingers holding his fork and knife as he sliced his piece of pork into two last bites. The Boogaloo I had known lived a life of hard work, drinking,

16

travel, a life filled with so much work and travel, overcrowded with sun, sweat, drinking, drying out.

> An ox jerking a wagon
> up a dusty red lane
> on the edge of a cane field
> his right hand catching
> the back of the wagon
> the force of the ox pulling
> the silver edge of the sideboard
> slicing off half his pinkie.
> A blood orange sun
> the silent tremble of sweat
> Changó
> screaming
> Changó
> grabbing his wrist
> Changó
> falling into the dusty lane

Let's go, Boogaloo. We'll walk along the shore for a bit before I leave.

Yes, it is a nice evening for a walk.

And good after such a fine meal, no?

Boogaloo nodded a thank you and we both stood. My hand fell to my right side, the bottle of hot sauce firm against my ribs, inside my coat pocket. We walked around the circle of birch trees and headed for the shore, Boogaloo humming a few verses of "The Dance of the Tired Ox." The sun was an orange globe on the other side of the lake, slowly giving way to the grayish blue dusk that arose on the beach. Boogaloo put his arm inside mine, holding on to my biceps. I put my hand over Boogaloo's, my feet twisting in the sand with each step, what was left of his missing pinkie smooth and soft.

The sun had dipped below the horizon, the lake a charcoal blue, the sky smudged with pink bleeding into an azure that slowly darkened the farther I looked away from the horizon. Boogaloo stopped, his purple scarf fluttering up near his left ear, its color deepening all the blue we stood amidst.

Boogaloo said, I don't know what you do . . . I mean for work, Ernestito, I don't know that kind of work. But I have a feeling that some days you think it is too easy, you don't feel good for all you do.

We stood just short of the water, the waves white and loud, rushing with sand and stones. Two children, their heads covered by their yellow slickers, ran along the edge of the waves, a flock of seagulls swerving up above them, screeching. Their father threw an orange float tied to a long white rope out into the sea, a black Lab running into the waves and paddling out to retrieve it. The children ran away into the darkening blue, their mother following close behind.

Don't feel this way—don't feel bad, Boogaloo told me.

I nodded, turned my head down, dragged the tip of my shoe through the moist sand, tracing an *E*, scratching it out, and following with half an arc.

Good work is good work. And remember that your father is now going into the dark. He needs to see some light, no?

We stared at each other.

Escúchame, hijo: don't forget your father . . .

Boogaloo stopped, his hand raised to his mouth.

How you say it, ante de memoria? You know, after memory?

Yes, after, but you might also mean *before*, or maybe *more*. No?

Segudo. You know what I mean. We have to live ante de memoria . . . We live with more than memory.

My stomach was full and warm; I felt like a child who had filled himself with a scrumptious meal before bed. I liked how Boogaloo called me hijo; for once it felt right, not mean but filled with concern, perhaps even a kind of respect. I repeated to myself what he had said: *Don't forget your father.*

I remembered then the time we couldn't find any work. The days were cold and wet, too cold for summer, and July seemed to pass in a silver mist. Boogaloo drove us farther north than we had ever been. Finally, Boogaloo stopped at a blueberry patch. We—Boogaloo, my father, and me—were paid thirty-five cents for each pound we picked. Boogaloo and my father could bring in five dollars after a fast day of work, their pants soaked to the knees from walking down the rain-filled paths, brushing against the bushes, the patch bathed in a thick fog. I was lucky to make a dollar fifty, maybe two; it took me forever to pick a pound of blueberries. I worked with a water cooler at my side, trying to stay in the patch as much as possible, peeing when I needed to, drinking water and eating blueberries so I wouldn't lose any time. Everything was wet, water everywhere I turned, my hands red and raw from so much water, so that I suddenly came upon an idea: I could have a pound of blueberries much faster if I poured a little water from the cooler into the tin of blueberries. No one seemed to notice, and for a few days I left the patch with a dollar or so more.

One day I slipped on the muddy path and cut my right hand on the thick, gnarled trunk of a bush, my hand wet with blood and mud when I arose from the path. I wiped my hand on the front of my pants. I started filling an empty pail with water to soak and clean my hand when the manager of the patch, a short heavy woman in a green rain poncho and red boots yelled out, Well, I think we found the one who's putting all the water in the berries. She told me to get my things together and come up front. They called Boogaloo from the patch; my father was asleep in the car, shivering with fever and too much drink. We stood on the edge of the patch, the manager pulling off the hood of her poncho and talking to her husband, who weighed the blueberries and packed them. Boogaloo stood next to me, a half-filled pail of blueberries in his hand. She explained about the water, handed Boogaloo and I a dollar, and then she told us we had to go. She and her husband turned and walked down the lane toward the small lean-to where the berries were weighed.

Boogaloo pulled his pail back and flung the blueberries out into the air, a stream of blue cutting through the mist—his gesture quick, light, and with such grace that I didn't understand how he suddenly stood in front of me. He swung the pail and struck me on the side of the head, and my ears filled with the bright tin and my face was hot and pulsed with a sharp pain. Boogaloo looked at me with great disgust, his jaw clenched, his lips turning up, his eyes black and deep. He said things; I couldn't hear anything for the ringing in my head. And then he punched me in the stomach, and when I doubled over I heard ¿*Tu me entende?* Never, never give up work, Ernestito. Work is work.

I closed my eyes for a moment, my fist crumpling the dollar tightly. When I opened my eyes, Boogaloo had disappeared. My head was hot with sweat, my shoulders beginning to shake in the wet, cold air. I tucked the crumpled dollar into my pants pocket. When I raised my hand to wipe away the sweat from my face, I realized I was shaking with tears and my hand was soaked with blood.

Now Boogaloo touched the side of my face with his open palm, his dark work-worn hand soft.

I am sorry, Ernestito.

I thought, I'll never forget what happened, and just at that moment the side of my face felt like it was on fire. I wanted to tell him: *You had no right or reason to hit me back then, Boogaloo, and I'll always remember the taste of that tin pail.* But instead I said, Thank you, Boogaloo, thank you for everything.

He tried to smile, held up his hand as if to push my thanks away, a big tear dropping from his right eye.

No, *listen*: thank you, Manuel Perez.

And before he could say anything I raised my hand up to his neck, tucking the fluttering end of his scarf under the collar of his coat. In that moment I had to let him know I knew his name; that Manuel Perez was not lost in all that blue.

Ernestito, no matter who we believe we were, or what we think we have done, we have to live . . .

He took hold of my hand and kissed my palm.

I squeezed his shoulder. I wanted to say, *I forgive you, Manuel.* Those words never came, and instead I said, I find many days, many, many days, where I don't know what to do. I looked down at the sand, and then looked him in the eyes. I haven't talked to them in so long . . . What can I say? Why will they want to talk to me?

My nose filled with sharp pain as my eyes filled with tears. Boogaloo held my hand tighter, and I didn't cry.

Maybe no one will have anything to say or do, Ernestito. But you never know. You can only do what you can do.

There was a dark blue streak of sky behind Boogaloo, then both our heads turned toward the bass tremble of a distant foghorn. I felt the darkness of the sea beginning to rise all around us.

Boogaloo said, You have your daughter to think of now.

I jerked my hand away, hugged myself tightly, bit down hard on my teeth.

My daughter?

Yes, Isabel, he said, without any hesitation or wonder. Magdalene's never loved anyone but you, everyone knows that, hijo. How can you not know Isabel is yours?

Boogaloo touched my cheek briefly, shrugged.

Isabel would soon turn five . . . My legs trembled and I could only think of the years that had passed, of my not knowing, even though Isabel and Magdalene were never that far away from me. And then, *Magdalene took Isabel to Puerto Rico because she knew I was her father, and now they are miles and miles away.* The dog down the beach barked, and then the children laughed, followed by the deep bellow of the foghorn and the waves crashing into the shore. I had tried to stay in touch with Magdalene. One day out of the blue, after I had gone into the world on my own, she wrote to me and asked if I would meet her on Mackinac Island. We spent a wonderful weekend together, one of the best times of my life, and after I left her up there I wrote Magdalene a letter or a card once a month for the next nine, and when she never answered I tried to call her. I tried and tried; I wanted deeply to be a part of her life. She never called back or wrote. She seemed to be ignoring me, and though I couldn't understand why, I finally left her alone.

I took Boogaloo's hand again; I needed it; I was confused, the swirling blues and grays of the evening causing me to shake and swerve as I tried to walk. I had to find a new path—*how could I cross the distance that kept me and Magdalene and Isabel apart?*

Just in front of his cabin Boogaloo stopped. He said, If I could do it all over again, I'd do anything to know my daughter.

Your daughter?

Yes. She never knew me. And it's probably too late for me but not for you, Ernestito.

My daughter, Isabel. What will she know or say of me? And then I saw her and Magdalene standing under a mango tree, their legs and feet streaked with red dust; and when they turned to me, hummingbirds in purple and green circled around them.

We took a few steps closer to the cabin. I said thank you once again, and when I went to say more, Boogaloo put two fingers up to his lips to quiet me. I heard sand striking the porch with a small yet sharp sound. Boogaloo pointed to the sea with his hand, his fingers sweeping back the waves, almost as if he could stop or part them, and then I understood he was saying *Go, go away*.

He told me, Your father and I never got it right; we didn't know how— or were never given the chance—to be fathers. You have to learn for yourself what that means, Ernestito. But you can make a lot fewer mistakes than us.

His hand was still in the air, and once again he pointed to the sea, his fingers waving me backward toward the waves. Boogaloo opened the door to his cabin and stepped inside. A light came on, gold behind the curtains. The wind picked up strong and shook the rum bottles hanging on the porch, their clapping along with the sound of the foghorn, and I heard the blues of this evening, the surging melody of a newfound feeling: *Isabel, Magdalene*.

Boogaloo had waved me away. Go, go away. He wasn't saying good-bye; he was telling me, showing me: *Go, go away across the sea. As fast as you can—go*. Boogaloo's figure, outlined by the golden light, was seated next to his table. I heard him turn on the radio, a soft trumpet sketching a ballad.

I turned back to the sea. Boogaloo had offered me the chance to go, but back then on that March day the sea seemed so dark and wide, stretched by miles and miles and miles, and though I should have run as fast as I could and jumped in, I turned away from the sea, and the waves continued to crash with its memory and remorse, and Magdalene and Isabel were still thousands of miles away, across an even vaster sea.

Boogaloo's ashes were housed in an eight-by-ten cardboard box. Gently rocking it in my palms, I felt Boogaloo dancing, heard the sweet sound of salsa, *Ay, que suave*, Boogaloo's strong, hard torso black and shiny in the sun, his shirt wrapped around his head, Boogaloo dancing on the edge of a potato field, golden dust springing from his shoes and powdering the air. Ever since I had claimed his ashes, I had this need to keep Boogaloo close by, safe, while I figured out what to do with his death.

I placed the box on the windowsill next to an empty canning jar. Shadows fell through the window, the sound of feet running through the grass. The walls of this migrant shack were bare, the wood cracked and stuffed in places with bright pieces of wool and balled-up newspaper. On the floor, a twisted mattress, half of it wet, the other half torn open; its insides puffy, pouring out into a thick yellow mound. A single bulb hung above a table, the outer figure of the bulb black with soot. There were no chairs, or a refrigerator, or a stove, but there were three blue cups, a white plate, an empty coffee can, and a small trail of crumbs on the table. A milk crate sat on the floor just off the edge of the table, almost as if someone had recently eaten here. Out in the orchard, voices, laughter; inside, the floor creaking in places and turning soft, then becoming hollow and hard as I stepped into the doorway.

I looked up, squinted, following the blue sky beyond the trees, and then found the sun beginning its slow descent.

Children zigzagged back and forth across the orchard lane, yelling under the trees brimming with blossoms. There was music in the air along with the distinct smells of cherries, cinnamon, coffee. Migrant workers, farmers, city folks, tourists—all had gathered to celebrate May Day. John Lindquist stood on a makeshift stage presenting red and blue ribbons to students from the local schools. The crowd clapped. A boy waved a ribbon over his head, smiling. *Renaldo Lacasa*. He waved the ribbon higher, with more flair, ecstatic with accomplishment, and I smiled and waved back, stepping from the doorway onto the orchard lane. I nodded to Mrs. and Mr. Lacasa, both of them filled with pride. I slid my hands into my pockets, turning my head downward, the orchard lane worn smooth and bare. Renaldo rushed over to me.

Standing there in short pants and sandals, a striped purple and yellow T-shirt, Renaldo shyly held the ribbon in his palm. I crouched down, took the ribbon from him, and pinned it to his T-shirt with the ribbon's small golden clasp. I stood and shook my fist in solidarity, a gesture that always elicited a response.

First place, Ernestito, he said. He lifted the coarse vanilla paper.

Excellent, Renaldo. I held the paper at arm's length as Renaldo and his parents looked on. Renaldo had painted the landscape as if he had stood above the countryside looking down on the city, the streets, his school, the freshwater sea, the cannery his father worked in.

Pointing at the watercolor, I said, Renaldo, and this little bay, the road, the boy on the bicycle . . .

Yes, here—Renaldo pointed with quick excitement, the bodily shift of recognition—my blue harbor and my sea road. I love to ride this way and look out on the boats, the sea, the harbor.

He laughed, then suddenly stopped himself, perhaps self-conscious of my understanding. I immediately heard memories of another sea road, some other blue released into our *now*.

Ah, yes. I see the blue is its own. It is a blue different from all the rest. It's *your* azul, Renaldo.

I unfolded the thick white paper dusted with cinnamon, the paper smudged and flecked with brilliant henna highlights, vivid in the late-afternoon light.

A colleague and I spent our Thursday afternoons at a local arts center helping elementary and high-school students with various projects; she often shared diverse forms of art and music; I, an array of literary works and documents. Out of all the students who had worked over the winter and spring to get their projects ready for the festival, it was Renaldo who had created countless drafts, who always had a sense of beginning again, who waited for something to appear, for something to happen. Renaldo seemed to relish the depth of a page; he followed the bold letters and lines, traced the strange curves of blue and red, and the squiggly ornament of green and black lines on the top edges of letters he studied in old volumes. Sometimes we simply left the arts center behind, left books upside down or open to the sun, left our brushes wet with paint, our hands streaked and splotched, a whole group of students walking out into the winter afternoon, the air freezing the paint hard on our hands. We walked into the woods looking at the light take shape on the snow, listening to the creaking, ice-covered trees. I stopped on a ridge, the sheen of the distant, open sea blue on the horizon, knelt down, showed Renaldo the silver fur of a rabbit torn and fluffy on the snow, the little drops of blood, the imprint of a hawk's wing.

Renaldo had taken all this in and waited for something to swoop down on him—and, now, I held it in my hands. The paper unfolded like a map, into four panels revealing long whitewashed walls. Around the borders of the walls he had painted lavender flowers, tall stalks of cane, and thorny pineapples. Then the imprint of something swooped down on me. Magdalene had been teaching before I ever started; I never told her this, but she was my model, my hero, and what she accomplished helped me to imagine my possibilities as a teacher. If she were here, Magdalene and I could have worked at the arts center together. Isabel could have said: *My father works with books. My mother, too.* And Magdalene and Isabel could be standing here with me now, looking at Renaldo's work.

Marvelous, Renaldo, just marvelous. I squeezed his shoulder, Renaldo's face reddening with embarrassment and pride.

Inside the border of flowers, cane, and pineapples, Renaldo had created walls where he had written poems. He had composed the poems himself. He had composed them in the words he had heard from his mother and father, from his memories of Cuba; they were poems inspired by the words of those poets who had most moved him in this first winter here, this first year away from his island home. And between two poems about his abuela, Renaldo had placed a photograph: Renaldo and his mother and father standing on the edge of a runway, a white plane behind them. Fat, heavy-looking bags pulled down his parents' shoulders. Their faces were mournful, composed of severe smiles as they waved. Renaldo stood between them, his eyes staring wide and hard, filled with dark fright, a small book cradled in his arm.

I carefully folded the paper. Mrs. and Mr. Lacasa came closer.

You have a great talent here, I said, looking into Mrs. and Mr.'s eyes.

Es un poeta.

They nodded, smiling. Mr. Lacasa shook my hand. Mrs. Lacasa put her arm around Renaldo.

Will you sit with us, Ernest?

Sure.

I turned to give Renaldo his walls of poetry, his watercolor.

He shook his head.

No . . . No, Renaldo I can't . . .

I want you to have it, Ernest, for helping.

Mrs. and Mr. Lacasa told me with their eyes that the gift was mine.

Thank you, Renaldo, thank you.

Renaldo took my right arm, his mother my left, his father's hand on my back, and like a small parade we marched off toward the crowd gathered around the stage. There were bowls of cherries, plates of cheeses, bottles of wine and juice, and blankets spread across the field in a confetti of colors. The crowd looked up toward the frame of purple curtains that adorned the stage.

We sat down. Mr. Lacasa handed me a short glass of wine. We clinked glasses. We shared sliced mango, strong goat cheese, crispy French bread.

Would you like some rice and beans? Mrs. Lacasa asked.

Yes, I nodded, my eyes widening.

A short man in a dark green khaki uniform walked to the front of the stage, a blue blowtorch in his hand, a long orange and yellow flame rising just above his head. Tree warmers brought in from the orchard lanes were placed around the perimeter of the crowd. The man in the green uniform bent down in front of one, and then there was a loud *wooofff*, followed by flames appearing in the warmer. People clapped. He lit another. *Wooofff.* More clapping. And then another. The heat from the warmers pushed in toward us, barely visible clouds of warmth beginning to take shape in the air and to surround the larger field of memory we were sitting within. Out here, in this orchard, families had gathered into a community of work, wages, food, and celebration. Some picked cherries. Some stirred vats filled with cherries. Some stacked cases of cherries. To some, I was much better off and quite different than these families. I was an oddity—a solitary man, unmarried, without friend or family, a rare bird who almost always walked

26

around in a black suit (perhaps the most casual memory someone had of me was of a warm evening, my shirt sleeves rolled to my elbows, my tie tucked into my breast pocket, pitching a softball in the bottom of the seventh inning, my white shirt and black pants streaked with red dust). I was extremely fortunate; I had been given the opportunity to teach writing at a small fine-arts school, but somehow I had also become a part of the larger life of this community: a man who worked as a teacher, who sometimes helped workers fill out forms, sometimes helped to organize events for this May Day festival, sometimes started a softball game in an orchard.

I wasn't that alone, though. I had Boogaloo. What to do with him, I thought, is something I still need to come to terms with. *I must live with Boogaloo a little longer*. Then I can tell my father, I can tell Magdalene all I hope for her and Isabel—for them, within my life.

Mrs. Lacasa asked, What about your family, Ernesto? You were born here, no?

I watched the shifting orange flames of a heater for a moment, heat rising up into the air, and then I crossed my legs at the ankles and held my knees.

Yes, I was born in Michigan. My father answered a call for work and came here to work at a mushroom cannery. That's when he met my mother.

I rocked back and said, About fifteen years ago they moved to Puerto Rico; it was always my father's dream to go back.

How are they doing?

Okay, I guess.

You say that as if you don't know, or don't talk to them, Mr. Lacasa said. He was lying on his side, his head propped up with one hand, Renaldo leaning back on his chest.

You are right . . . I don't talk to them. I . . . I stopped, looking up into the darkening sky that still held blue and was tinted with the orange of the evening's sun.

You think you are the bad son, Ernesto? Mr. Lacasa asked.

I guess so. They moved far away. I was happy for them, but I think, too, I have a hard time understanding their choices, or even my own, I said. And then: They had some hard times. I don't know how they can still be together, why their love stayed so strong.

Hmmm . . . Mr. Lacasa took a drink of his wine, and I raised my glass to my lips, looked at Mrs. Lacasa, and then said, I'm the bad son because I avoided them, I tried to forget them, and now I'm too ashamed to . . .

There was a small pocket of silence, as if the warmth of the burners had surrounded us, quieting our voices, our thoughts.

Nonsense, Mrs. Lacasa said. Everything you might have done may seem the acts of a bad son, but all you are doing now might be that of a good son.

Sí, sí, it is true, Mr. Lacasa said.

We all turned, and four children walked out across the stage, big silver stars tied to the front of their bodies, their arms raised high in the air. They had brought out the night, and in their brief presence we were to experience the unfolding darkness within the sanctuary of their brightness. Mr. Lacasa raised Mrs. Lacasa's hand, palm open, to his lips.

My brother went away to England for almost twenty years, Mrs. Lacasa began, and without a word except maybe a postcard every five years or so. One afternoon, after a heavy rain, the trees still wet and the red road full of mud, Papí points, screams, Ay, mijito. We saw a man walking next to the cane field, his arms and face pale like a ghost against his yellow guayabera. My father and mother walked, almost running, as fast as they could toward my long-lost brother, Javier. Tears were streaming down their faces, but they were so happy, she said.

Everything quieted. She wiped her face with the back of her arm, and Renaldo came over and sat in her lap. She hugged him and kissed the side of his neck.

I remember Papí kept saying Javier must have walked for days, mile after mile, pointing to his feet, and we couldn't see Javier's boots because they were caked in hard red mud, and his pants were soaked and clung to his knees.

The stars began walking off the stage, and I saw underneath those stars an evening when Mrs. Lacasa's memory would become part of a story we would return to because we needed to tell it to one another—a story I would tell, hoping Isabel and Magdalene would come and sit by me.

White paper birds suddenly appeared on the edge of the purple curtains, fluttering above us. Following the birds was a young boy who was the sun, who helped everyone see the new morning of this play.

Excuse me, I have to go for a moment. I stood up, and then, caught in the heat of the tree warmers, I glimpsed my own arms, no longer pale but reddened by the sun of this May Day.

I'll be right back.

They nodded. I turned away, rolled my shirtsleeves back down, buttoned them, and found a path through the crowd, my eyes intent on the shack, on going to get Boogaloo.

Ernest, tell me what you are most afraid of.

Magdalene, is that you?

Please . . .

I heard ice cubes clinking in a glass, a deep sigh on the other end of the line.

Please, don't ask any questions. Just answer me, tonight, in this moment, please talk to me.

Magdalene . . . Lots of things scare me. The edges of dark trees at night, for instance. Certain storms where . . .

No, no. I mean, what scares the hell out of you, deep in your heart-of-hearts, Ernest. What're you most afraid of? Give it to me straight.

Magdalene lets out a long breath, a humming melody following behind.

Do you remember that time when we first met, when I started the fifth grade in Niles after my father brought me back from Puerto Rico?

Yes.

There's static, silence, then the distinct sounds of coquis in the background.

On that day I was afraid of everyone I had to meet, of starting at a new school. They separated me from the rest of the class for part of that day. I guess, looking back, they wanted to make sure I wasn't a migrant kid from the fields who needed special help. You were so nice to me; I knew I had found a friend.

For a moment I pause, turn to the fruit crate on the floor filled with books and papers, an alarm clock on top. It's one fifteen in the morning. The light outside my window dark blue; Boogaloo's last words come to me again from that blue.

I am afraid of . . . I want to make sure, I guess, that I never separate anyone like that. If they need me, all they have to do is ask.

I pause, give her time to say anything. Silence. I finally say: The feeling of that day, my nauseous stomach, shaky arms—I never want to cause that feeling.

Yes. Maybe you don't want others to feel alone.

Maybe . . . and maybe I'm trying to say I'm afraid of a feeling I've had for a long time: I'll never have a friend again.

I want to tell her more, I want to tell her I know Isabel is my daughter . . .

You will—don't worry; I bet you'll have plenty of friends. You know what I'm afraid of?

Tell me.

That I was never the friend you remember.

Don't talk that way, Magdalene. Your were—still are—even if you're far away.

The coquis suddenly grow louder, almost as if Magdalene has dropped the phone amid a grove of trees.

How's Isabel?

She's great. I think she loves it here.

I can easily imagine she does—the colors of flowers, too, the shaking palms, Abuela holding her hand as they walk down a narrow cobblestone street. She loves these things and even more.

And you?

She laughs, with a forced air to it, her voice filled with phlegm, then there's the clinking of ice cubes again.

Fine, fine, fine. She hiccups, giggles. Perfecto. Isabel loves it and so do I, in a way. What can I say: I'm seeing a place I knew nothing about, and I'm discovering my memory.

She hiccups again. Hey, remember that August you visited me up on Mackinac Island?

Of course, it was one of the best times in my life.

Don't say that.

Why not? It's the truth. Remember all the letters I wrote?

Magdalene doesn't answer, and I try to tell it as straight as I can.

You never wrote me back. Some letters were returned. And then the next spring, I knew you'd have a break before your new teaching job in the fall, and so I called your parents' but never reached you. You were never home. Your mother told me that maybe I should realize you didn't want to talk to me.

She did?

Yes.

That bitch. Ernest, I never said anything to her, I didn't even know you called. And I read your letters . . . those that I got. I was afraid of what they said, what they might mean for your life.

They only meant what they said—how I felt about you. And I called again, right around Christmas; your mother said you didn't live with them anymore. I called once more. She told me you moved in with Juan.

I'm so sorry that we never talked. She must be taking a long drink. I hear her catching her breath.

There were many fallen and growing leaves, Magda. My seasons of trying to talk to you.

She asks, Wasn't that the song we played over and over again, "Straight, No Chaser"? You said you had a movie in your mind, following to a T the exact arc of the song . . . Two people talking straight.

Yes, we played it—but the song we played the most was "Milestones (Alternate Take)"—that was the song, and its length is 5:59. And then remember we switched to Coltrane's "Lush Life"?

My God, what a memory! I hear it now. Listen. Really, Ernest, that time up there was one of your best?

Absolutely.

Would you be afraid to meet there again?

No. This summer, maybe. And then I see the chance I need: Yes, August again. You and Isabel can . . .

The static is crazy on the line.

Listen, Ernest, I hear Isabel; I need to go. I'll tell everyone you said hi.

Are you sure?

Yeah, I gotta go.

Magdalene?

Yes.

Make sure you remember that tonight I said hello. Remember it this way: you called, to return my letters and calls from back then.

Bye.

I set the phone down, pull the blanket away from my legs. I stand up and shiver in the cold. Outside, the field is silver blue in the moonlight. I pat the box on my desk housing Boogaloo. I slip on the sweater draped over my chair, slide my feet into a pair of sandals, and walk outside. I feel like I might retch, my stomach filled with . . . filled with the simple awareness of my aloneness in this moment, in this field, surrounded by blue, and in the distance the never-ending sound of the freshwater sea. How for someone with so much time it continues to leave me more and more alone. When my parents got back together that last time, after being apart twice, I didn't understand them. One day I saw them leaving a movie theater. I stood underneath a tree and watched them. They were quiet, holding hands, walking past a small fountain, unaware of my presence.

Their love is a mystery, a force I'm simply afraid to understand. Things can change in a moment's notice. Five minutes and fifty-nine seconds, an alternate take, new milestones.

Magdalene's discovering her memory—good for her.

A breadfruit thudding against the ground. A bone-skinny dog nudging a bottle across an empty plaza. The azure sea. Palm trees scratching together. The sun disappearing behind a cloud. My father standing under a tree singing. The sea's breeze stirring a pink mosquito net. A copy of the first poem I wrote while attending La Escuela Católico de Anasco. Abuela cooking in her kitchen, swaying and singing as she seemed to float from the table to the stove.

These memories stay with me, they color my dreams, and I hope Magdalene and Isabel discover those memories that will bring some shape and form to their lives, that will bring them home. Magdalene and Isabel can color my dreams and memories, too.

Things can change. New milestones. I cross the silvery blue field, the grass moist with dew. A deer lifts its head, flicks its tail, and then disappears in a silent leap into the trees. The wind shivers their branches, the birches a bright white in the moonlight. I can smell the sea, wet stones, pines moving in the wind, and my hands shake with a strange feeling, like waves returning, one after another, after another . . .

When Lorime was beaten on the edge of the bridge, in the little circle of grass where the city had placed a flagpole and bronze cannons in memory of World War II veterans, he was about to cross to the other side, perhaps on his way to visit me. Sometimes I would tell Magdalene how I was filled with shame when I realized I had not remembered Lorime. His nose had been broken when he was thrown against the bridge, and his skull was fractured, too, but that's not what killed Lorime. He died later that evening of internal bleeding. Downstream, sitting drunk under a mulberry tree, the river flowing by, filled with the setting sun, I never knew he was being beaten by four young men, or that he had been taken to the hospital, where he died, even though I had looked up when I heard the sirens on the bridge. We were all—Juan, Magdalene, and me—responsible for Lorime's death. We were aware he was effeminate, and when we called him linda, homey, and, sometimes, preciosa, little by little we contributed to his death. The young men who beat him didn't have the same laughter and love we had, but our words helped to name Lorime in the terms they needed for their actions.

I'll always remember the smell of fall-cut grass—manure, a hint of honey and rain, the wilted flowers of a cold sun—whenever I recall Lorime's death. A bright, endless sky, clouds like islands drifting by in a sea of soft azure, and the sound of the river tumbling over the dam upstream.

Somehow, in those smells and colors of grass and earth and water and sky, I felt something that brought love and hate together.

Lorime, I sometimes can't hear the river without the sirens, without tu cada linda in the sun.

I need to turn this pain into something just on the edge of forgiveness, and I should have said to Magdalene on the phone: Magdalene, I can't live without tu cada linda in the sun.

Please, come home to me soon, my friend, *I yell to the birches, the deer, the sea,* and bring our daughter with you.

I have written three passages for Isabel, and I've sealed each one in a separate, cream-colored envelope. They might be conceived as letters, but they are actually passages to myself because they are small boats taking me through a sea of time, and in each one I hold on dearly—pushing past the high-rolling waves—because I don't want them lost. I want the urgency of each passage to be clear when Isabel needs them. And I want her (and Magdalene) to know I can travel away from my loneliness.

On the front of each envelope I've written *Isabel and Magdalene*, and I've sealed them with the blue wax imprint of a dolphin and an anchor. After writing each passage, I discovered they had an inevitable order; so above each waxed seal I've lightly penciled a number for that order.

The birch trees take in the warmth of the sun moving higher, away from the east, their spring leaves becoming shiny as I stand here looking out the window. Out past the trees, the freshwater sea is a choppy azure, and a lone fishing boat makes its way toward the islands, its long prow lifting above and then breaking through the waves. For the past few weeks the morning light has grown stronger, and this morning I turned off my lamp a little before six. There's a half-empty cup of coffee on my desk, a broken pencil, a fountain pen, and a pile of blue three-by-five cards—the passages needed to be remembered and discovered, and, ultimately, the morning light offered me the chance to invent their urgency before I transcribed them to sheets of paper. I pick up the three envelopes and place them within a larger envelope addressed to my father.

Five years ago, in the spring, when Magdalene finished her student teaching and I knew she'd have a break before her new job in the fall, I was hurt—a sudden incomprehensible weight in my stomach, my heart thick and uncontrollable in my throat—when her mother told me not to call again, that I should know by now Magdalene didn't want to talk to me. The previous winter I had ordered my passport in the hope of persuading Magdalene to travel to Spain; even though she had not returned my calls or letters, I felt this trip, if I could reach her and persuade her to go, might help her to understand how much I cared. Ever since I first met Magdalene she always had a worn copy of *Aesop's Fables* at her reach; I wanted us to visit the Prado and see Velázquez's stunning portrait of the maestro. With her words, Magdalene's mother smashed my dream.

I woke up one day alone in my apartment in Chicago, the window rattling from the El, and when the train passed and took its shadows with it I heard the robins crazy with May, and I decided I would go to Madrid alone. I wandered through the Prado for several mornings, studying Aesop's face, always a few feet back and to the side, reminded over and over again of that old white ox from my childhood in Puerto Rico; and I took in his eyes, pooled in the light of a clarity he seemed to have from within the sharp edges of life—a clarity, I decided, one finds in streams where the white and gray and black-flecked stones are, without doubt, round, perfect, and perfectly present. Looking at that portrait, I thought I understood the wealth of poverty. Up the hill from the Prado, I made my way to the Plaza Santa Ana in the afternoons, to drink beer or brandy and to eat small plates of tender anchovies in vinegar and tart meaty olives stuffed with blue cheese. It may have been about twelve years before that my parents had written and asked me to visit them in Puerto Rico. They had even offered to buy the ticket, and they mentioned I could stay as long as I liked, could consider living there. Their offer was too close to the past; it scared me. Back then, I was busy—beginning to make choices and changes; I decided to move to South Bend and go my own way. In Madrid I walked around in a dream, filled with awe and hunger as my childhood returned to me in a cobblestone calle dropping down a hill and filled with midday sunlight; in the iron balconies flowering from the clean mango-painted buildings; in a quiet, still plaza at dusk in that moment when the lamps ignite and become a part of the blue light; and in the faint strumming of a guitar coming from some piso. Sitting at a small table in that plaza, my hands resting between a short coffee and a copa of brandy, Madrid's evening sky seemed giant and endless. I listened to the guitar and felt I was exactly where I should be.

One morning I took a slow train into the mountains and granjas, and I spent my last three days walking the tight-shadowed and sun-patterned calles of Segovia. I stood next to the ancient wall of the alcázar, the river down below a deep, thick green, the countryside golden and dry and beautiful, my shoulders covered by an orange and red mantón I had bought from an old, sun-sharpened woman, those same colors woven into the rocks and stones and dirt that lay as far back as my memory and imagination could go. Near the center of town I sat without a sense of regret, looking at the aqueduct reflect a way I'll never know.

That solo trip must've been a part of my fate—even if I would have spoken to Magdalene, she could not have gone with me; that May, though I didn't know it then, she gave birth to Isabel.

Now I look at a photograph taken of me at the house of the poet Antonio Machado, who wrote these beautiful lines:

> The sorrows that turned
> my heart into a beehive
> today treat it
> like an old city wall,
> which they want to knock down, and soon,
> under the blows of a pickax.

I sit back down, and on the back of the photograph I write,

Dear Changó,

> I have gone far away
> as you also
> and now I return, looking ahead,
> and though I may not
> deserve it, I need
> your help. Please
> give these envelopes
> to Isabel and Magdalene.

Ernest

36

There was a sudden bang against my window. Two sparrows were fighting over a bit of red yarn, their wings fast and steady as they floated for a moment in the blue sun-shaped air, and then it was as if a window or a doorway had suddenly filled with light, and when I look into the light it is another morning, and I am sleeping under a blue mosquito net that flutters above me in the breeze. I roll to my side, sit up, and place my feet on the cool, smooth cement floor. Through the doorway I see my abuela at the end of the hall, standing in her kitchen, a silver spoon in her hand, and then she moves away and then returns, and I feel she's dancing and swaying in her kitchen, her flowered dress fluttering with her steps, Abuela dancing and swaying to music colored by the blue breeze stirring the mosquito net. I walk down the hall and listen to her spoon striking a pot, the smell of coffee and mangoes meeting my steps, and then Abuela's low yet strong humming.

Ay, Ernestito, sit down.

Abuela holds a blue bowl in her hands, a purple-throated humming-bird whirring above her silver hair. She puts the bowl down and turns to the sink, where she wets a cloth and wipes my face and eyes clean of sleep. She brings me the blue bowl filled with soft eggs, and then a small plate of cheese and bread and a steaming cup of coffee. Abuela stirs a teaspoon of sugar into the light coffee, stirs it fast, the spoon tapping against the inside of the cup. She lifts up the bread, tears it in half, and dips it into the soft eggs; the spongy white soaked with yellow and bits of black pepper. She hands me the piece of bread.

I never wondered where Changó was on that morning. Now, after years of continually returning to my abuela's brown hands around that blue bowl, I see that when Changó took me away to Puerto Rico it was some defining, true moment. When I first remembered that morning, I had an impulse to write the word *Awbela*, the immediate sound I heard when I saw her, and as I wrote the word down there arose the sounds and smells and tastes of things I thought I had erased forever. For some reason the eggs came back to me warm and peppery, the yellow cornmeal of the bread bleeding through. I would continue to return to the image of Abuela and feel my chest rise with something invisible and strong; the image helped me to live through the most dreadful days; there were hours in which I'd play it over and over in my mind from various angles—in the rain, on a bright sunny day, in the oddity of ice and snow falling in the tropics; and each time the words I told myself or wrote down on scraps of paper became more solid

37

and vivid and urgent as they leaped with fire; and the image became, as time passed, a compadre walking with me into various events and situations, at my side so that a moment would be utterly transformed: twelve hours of work in a noisy, hot factory becoming a morning of breakfast in a lush silence, a blue breeze, and the strong humming of Abuela's song.

I had to get the word—her name—just right. For years I tried to recreate the morning perfectly. There were so many years that I hadn't talked to my father, and without being aware of it I realized that in my mind he had become Father, even though I had never before called him Dad, Papa, Papí, or Father. Only Changó. What did that name mean to me? I learned of lightening and thunder, of dance and song, but how did the Changó that I remembered have anything to do with a god of music? I listened, tried to step into his rhythm; I heard his silence, the ways it was yoked to the power of his anger, how easy it seemed for Changó to punch the side of my head, strike my shoulders with the backside of a machete. How easy it was to pick up a bottle and take a long drink, and then smile, laugh, begin a song. And how he could ask me to stay with him, and why I stayed and went to the fields with him. That was of his music, too; that was all a part of our song.

I felt that I had no choice: I needed to perfect my memory of Abuela. Once the words and pictures—the word-pictures—were just right, I'd tell my father about that time, I'd discover a way to say—to name—what needed to be said between us.

It seemed like I had nowhere to turn. Sometimes, my life had its most immediate meaning when I saw it as close as pages in a book. *A beehive. An old city wall. A pickax.* There were things I wanted to express: the sound of a river on a morning so quiet the mist seemed to echo the river; a mango falling with a soft thud against the baked red-clay dirt; a hummingbird floating above a white orchid, the shimmering green of its body bleeding into the orchid each time it dipped its beak inside the flower's throat; the muscular, smooth passing of a paso fino horse on a road, its hooves like palms striking the skin of a conga drum. My father had created such a mysterious silence around language. And in my loneliness I searched for the opposite of that silence: if the pages of books were like fallen leaves scattered from a tree, I gathered them and found that when I brought them close together, I heard the smallest possibilities for both eliminating and deepening my father's silence.

Once, down on the river in my cabin, I was reading a book Magdalene had let me borrow when the rain startled me; raindrops spotted the cabin's sole window, and the spots reflected on the pages of the book, creating a blurry cursive between the black lines of words. In the book, a father is on his way to a wedding, where his daughter, who will die of AIDS, will be the bride. He's driving his fast motorcycle to the wedding and it has begun to rain. I found comfort in that connection, how the rains of our worlds meet. Later, that moment would help to justify a belief I was learning to substantiate with each day that passed: my life and world were as significant as any I encountered in a book.

The rain fell harder, its strumming heavy on the windowpane, and as I listened closer the script I thought I saw between the lines of words disappeared. Its impression stayed with me as the rain fell harder. I would learn that my story was as common as a man accelerating his motorcycle through a curve on a highway: a shy, quiet boy discovers wonder and solace in books. When he walks down the street on a sunny day reading a book, he can always look to his right and find company in the shadow, holding a book and walking through the sun with steady resolve. This story, my story, I finally realized, was filled with change, loss, and violence. Perhaps a kind of freedom, too: I was free to imagine and think and erase—if only temporarily—my memory. I could never escape the loss; I felt, in the end, I had to repair what had been violently ripped away. I had to discover why my father let me go out into the world without his help, why he let me go without his hand or his words.

Nothing is permanent. Life unfolds—in every instance, on its remarkable journey to who knows where—on a path of change. But things called to me, and I paid close attention, and once I immersed myself within them, like a hot piece of steel thrust into a bucket of clear water, I discovered a perfected permanence. When I surrendered to them—a leaf, a bird, a memory, a name, a stone wet with rain—I believed there was shape and reason and purpose for my life. I believed, if only within a moment's passing, that I was meant to build roads over the sea.

I place the photograph in the big envelope for my father and close it with its clasp, and then smooth a strip of tape over the flap. The sun is higher, farther to the west. A breeze has started; the undersides of the leaves shimmer like small silver discs. The sun falling through the window is warm on my arms, but I now slip on my sweater, pick up the envelope, and am on my way: I want to mail the envelope today, and then find a table outside and watch the sun move across Lake Michigan.

Part Two

Magdalene

Isabel is laughing, standing on an old Coca-Cola crate, stretching over the edge of the wooden table, and with a sugar spoon she scoops a small mixture of sliced Spanish olives and Scotch-bonnet peppers. She turns them onto a mound of mashed green bananas. Magdalene, looking through their bedroom window, cannot help but watch her daughter with envy; she helps the family make pasteles as if she has always lived with them. And the family seems to have accepted her without question.

Two weeks ago, without forewarning the family, they arrived in the dead of night, Magdalene walking in the door with a duffel bag over her shoulder, Isabel asleep in her arms. Magdalene's face full of strain, full of escape: running from a world where Juan Ríos, the man she had lived with, had died. And she knew, too, she was running from Ernest, the father of her child. At the funeral he stood in a black suit, dropping ferns into the grave. He hugged and kissed Isabel, the daughter he did not know was his.

Ernest's mother and father had said: This is Magdalene and her daughter, Isabel. They're from Michigan. She and Ernest were always such good friends.

Yet Magdalene thought she saw it in their eyes. They knew that Juan had died—*but why have she and Isabel come here?*

And then Ernest's mother said, She's Ramóna Crespo's daughter. *Remember her?*

She should never have tried to decide what was best. There was a feeling—brief and light—of a freedom to leave, to bring Isabel here and show her all the stories she had heard from Ernest, to show Isabel her father's memory. To see the memory and life she—Magdalene—had always dreamed: the island of her mother's birth. Now there are so many questions, so many questions and rumors she must bear.

She turns from the window, leans back against the cool wall, closes her eyes. Her father was born here, but she never learned who he was; no matter how many times she had asked her mother, she'd never tell her. Somewhere out on this island, she thinks, in a region I can't name, is the place—a barrio, a finca, a mountain, or a field?— where my father is from.

Why didn't her mother ever share this place with her? What did she hate so much, and what was she so afraid of?

Then there was that awkward moment of deep questioning in the family's eyes when she arrived: Why have you come here? Then the possible recognition: *Isabel is our blood*.

She steps through their bedroom door, closes it. The evening light soothes her eyes, her earlier throbbing headache now only a vague stroke in her brain, an ochre-throated hummingbird fluttering above an orchid on the edge of the patio painting her mind. She steps forward, the hummingbird hovering above her eyes, the sound of its wings a thundering of movement, and then it quickly disappears in a flash of red behind her. She crosses the small stone courtyard separating her and Isabel's room from the back portico. She stops in the doorway, her hands clasped behind her back.

Abuela holds a blackened pot against her waist, stirring mashed bananas with deep, slow folds, the pale-colored mash filled with thick swirls and rivulets.

Magdalene forces herself to stand back, this doorway a solid barrier. Her mother never talked of women like this, never spoke of this place, often told her to forget Puerto Rico—*It's dirty, they're dirty, and the sooner you forget about it, the better*. Magdalene is an outsider; she has no memories to offer this circle of women. It's easy for her to stand apart, to let Isabel create memories she can always return to, to let Isabel become a part of this family.

Abuela takes a banana leaf from the pile. She shows Isabel how to tear off the jagged, rough edges. She then smoothes the leaf flat with her palm on the table.

Abuela's daughter, Estella, pours a tablespoon of achiote oil onto the leaf. She slowly circles around the deep red oil. Estella lifts a mound of mashed bananas and heaps it onto the leaf. She pushes the middle down. Abuela fills the depression with a spoonful of goat stew. She looks into Isabel's eyes. Isabel stretches over the table, spoons up the olives and peppers, slowly adding these final ingredients. Evelyn, Ernest's mother, quickly folds the leaf over, folds once again, swiftly tucking under the ends. On the table is a small, dark bundle. Abuela ties it up with white string, Isabel helping as if they are putting the last careful touches on a Christmas present.

Singing rises from the cane field. All the women turn. Straw hats atop their heads, cradling forearm-lengths of sugarcane, Ernest's father, Changó; his grandfather, Abuelo; and Lillo, his great uncle, step from the field. Tucked inside the white string circling Lillo's hat—banana leaves, a rope cutting into his thick shoulders, a cluster of bananas banging against his buttocks. They're drenched in sweat, their clothes powdered with red dust. They remove their hats.

Everywhere she looks, all that she touches, smells, hears—mangoes falling to the soil, Isabel's soft brown skin, the blood red throat of a hummingbird fluttering over an orchid—all of it is filled with so much life, and not just Ernest's, but now she sees her own, too. His father stands lean, dark, and healthy looking from the sun, his hair matted against his skull, the only sign of a problem found in the deep dark sunglasses covering his eyes. He seems more open, talkative, a different man than the one Ernest talked about and who she remembered. He hasn't once shown any form of unkindness to Magdalene. But he could hate her; she's from Niles, her stepfather had been his boss at the cannery, and her mother . . . she had never said anything good about Ernest or Changó, and he knew it.

Changó walks over to the table, a small red banana between his fingers. He offers it to Isabel. Peeling away the red skin, she pinches off the end, lifts the soft fruit to Changó's mouth. Then she takes a bite. They both smile from the sweetness the banana exudes.

Magdalene can see that everyone seems happy, is in the presence of some kind of peace. Isabel laughs and licks her fingers. Lillo slings the bananas and rustling leaves over to the women. But Magdalene feels a swirling emptiness. Abuela strikes a silver spoon against the lip of a pot. There's a palpable silence, the soft touch of the world licking against Magdalene's face, yet not the embrace of warmth and love, the strength of two arms wrapped around her. She shivers.

Isabel is content with these women and men, with her family. But what of Ernest alone? Ernest, in need of his daughter, Isabel, laughing in his arms and knowing who her father is. Maybe Ernest would want Magdalene, too. The two of them embracing without having to justify or explain the anguish of their mutual pasts.

This family laughs, talks, and continues to work, showing Isabel their life and making her a part of it. They, too, feel Ernest's absence, but they go on. As if they know the whole story. As if one morning they will look out the window, see Ernest walking down the road, his loneliness a receding shadow drifting over the cane field.

The first night after Magdalene and Isabel arrived, the family went to a festival. There were many booths, displaying record-breaking sweet potatoes; bags of dark, rich coffee; red and yellow mangoes; systems of modern irrigation and fertilization imagined within the small blue streams, the thick trees, the rich green mountains, and the red clay dirt that someone had spun alive in miniature scale. The smell of seafood and roasting pork wafted in the air. Musicians played in the middle of the festival and men and women trembled with sweat as their hips swayed and bumped into each other. A swirl of orange taffeta and yellow silk, the flash of pink and blue.

Magdalene, Ernest's mother, and Abuela, holding Isabel's hand, walked along the craft tables. Abuela's sister-in-law, Iríke, had a booth with an array of crafts: colored hammocks, necklaces and bracelets made of seashells and almonds and stones, and watercolors of the sea and the mangroves. Iríke came from Loíza, where they weave hammocks and paint Yoruban masks. The masks were at the end of the table, animated in reds, greens, yellows, and blues. Some were filled with happiness, while others held a deep sadness. Isabel couldn't stop looking at the watercolors and necklaces showing the same image. Abuela and Iríke smiled. Iríke pulled out a white T-shirt with the same image in blue:

Magdalene watched as Isabel pulled the T-shirt over her head. She lifted the end and stared at the image as she twirled around. Abuela sat down in a chair and called Isabel to her lap. She looked at Magdalene, and then she turned to Isabel and told her that far above her barrio, up near the top of the mountain, on the shore of a clear-running stream that ran all the way to the sea, there was a round stone imbedded in the soil, and the stone held the same image as the T-shirt. Long ago, the Tainos had carved it there. A baby had been born with its face twisted in pain, and the mother finally understood her discomfort. Throughout her pregnancy the baby must have cried and cried, kicked and kicked, and this is why she never stopped peeing. The Tainos had carved the image to let us know we should be happy, and even though a life without sadness is incomplete, sadness must be washed away.

Isabel buried her face in Abuela's neck and clung to her tightly. And Magdalene walked forward and did so, too. As they held each other, Magdalene could feel that Abuela was telling the story of Ernest, and of other children who had lived in pain, those who had died: Lorime and Juan. Abuela called them *miniños de las ruinas*. Her soft words echoed within Magdalene, took on a life of their own, repeating themselves over and over: *these children, our ruins, our children of ruin.*

From afar, approaching the festival, they could hear sirens. Everyone rose from their booths and stared. Abuela guided Isabel to her feet, stood up, and led them down the aisle.

Abuelo and Ernest's father were standing in a circle of people, everyone animated, their voices low and whispered. Lying on the street, his dusty brown hair cradled in his elbow, was a dirty, tired-looking young man. Magdalene could tell he was young. His body was still growing, his hands soft, his eyelids smooth as if he were a boy sleeping under a tree on a lazy afternoon. Next to his outstretched hand was a clear, empty bottle of rum. He had on a pair of black leather boots that zipped on the side; one was unzipped, his bare foot sticking halfway out. His heel was dried and cracked with old blood. The sirens wailed down the street. She knew then that the young man was dead. The low whispers of the crowd rose. Ernest's father said the young man had been drinking and celebrating. He spent the afternoon dancing in the street so much that he was in need of a rest, and everyone thought he was taking a little nap.

A man in a shirt and tie checked the young man's pulse. He pulled the bottle away from his fingertips and laid a yellow plastic blanket over the body. Everyone had forgotten about Isabel. They only heard her crying, her voice rising above everyone else's: *Juan! Juan!*

And then she went silent, her mouth caught open, her eyes wide and deep black, tears streaming down her cheeks. It was as if she had stopped breathing.

Magdalene didn't know what to do.

Abuela lifted Isabel away from the dead man and repeated, *No llora, don't cry, don't cry, my little one*, rubbing Isabel's cheeks with her hand to coax her into catching her breath.

For the first time in a long time, Magdalene felt unsure of herself, felt how weak she could be, how she might not make it through her aloneness. The voices of the crowd pained her. Isabel's mouth wide open, her eyes shut tight, tears streaming down her cheeks.

Overhead, a plane thundered through the sky, then went silent. Magdalene watched the blinking red light, like her heartbeat pulsing across her eyelids, the blinking red the only life in the black sky. She ran to the sea.

The mangroves rustled in the warm, soft breeze, waves pounding against the shoal and ruffling back on their return. She could hear the music from the festival beginning once again. Out past a small island thick with mangroves, lit by the plumage of sea birds white in the starlight, the sea swirled with glittering phosphorescence. The birds shrieked, the sea shimmering with the rhythm of the birds. She believed that Isabel would not ask, or know, what had happened to Juan. But Isabel had seen the dead young man and called for him.

They had buried Juan three weeks ago: Magdalene and Isabel, her mother and her stepfather, the priest, and the undertaker. Ernest, who'd arrived late. That was all. A pair of crows overhead. All the black, bare trees, and a warm breeze for December, dried leaves rustling against gravestones. Isabel had never called him Father, or Dad. Never Papí. Only Juan. They never corrected her. They both knew Ernest was her father. Juan, at first, would flinch, for a moment, then open his arms wide.

Was there something Isabel knew? How will I ever answer her? *I was foolish and I didn't think of you, I thought of . . .*

When they were young, just before dark, Ernest would ride over on his bike. Magdalene playing hopscotch in her blue plaid dress, white socks, her shiny Mary Janes. The bike—like a velocipede, a blue iron horse; the thick tires, flowing handlebars, the leather saddle, and the word Presidents, *in*

white, down its withers. Ernest stops and she jumps on the handlebars.
They ride down Third Street to Bond, past Ring Lardner's home—the
river, the island, the mulberry trees—the river valley gleaming below, her
screams piercing the wind rushing past their descent of the Bond Street
hill. The leaves on the trees turning silver. The strips of shredded bark rus-
tling. Across the footbridge, the smacking slats of wood, the river pound-
ing the rocks below the dam, and then onto Parkway Avenue, underneath
the arching oak trees, the crunch of acorns below their speed. Ernest's
hands bumping against her thighs and the cool steel of the handlebars
tucked under her behind—once around Island Park, down Parkway, and
over the Broadway Bridge to Third.

Home. The brevity of those bike rides—how simple, their life circling
into itself. Neither she nor Ernest knew that the lonely cabin they passed
on Parkway would one day be Ernest's home; or the site of her most vivid
memories. Ernest sitting on an apple crate. The odor of vomit. Alcohol
seeping from his pores. Silent, tired, looking too dirty, too old. For only
seventeen, he looked ready to die.

Lillo takes Magdalene's hand. He gives her a cup of the cane juice he has just squeezed. His hands rise to her cheeks, and she feels the warmth his hands possess from working as he holds her face for a moment and then kisses her lightly.

The cane juice is sweet, thick, strange—her tongue, her throat, stumble to understand the newness of a juice she has never drunk. The women still work at the pasteles. There is now barely any sun falling over the back of the portico, so the breadfruit trees take on a deep, blackened green. The cows in the back field have become shadowy blurs, the air sparkling with fireflies. The coquis have begun their nightly chorus. Abuelo drops the green, white-string-tied bundles into a boiling pot of water. There is also a pot of arroz con gandules simmering on the stove. Ernest's father and Lillo sit on crates, drinking cane juice and talking.

Magdalene watches Isabel's hair swinging. There's mashed banana on the ends. Abuela laughs and hugs her. Tía Estella continues to turn circles with the red oil. The pot on the stove boils a white stream of smoke into the darkening evening.

Mamí, Isabel calls. She takes Magdalene's hand and yanks her from the door to the table. Tía Estella dribbles a spoonful of achiote oil onto a banana leaf. Abuela scoops to the leaf a mound of bananas and pushes it in. Magdalene catches Abuela's hand. She takes the spoon and turns the goat stew onto the mound of bananas. Isabel lifts her head with that quizzical look: *Hey, how'd you know?* Magdalene takes Isabel's hand, and together they plop on top the sliced peppers and olives, the final ingredients.

Magdalene turns to Ernest's mother. Evelyn begins to fold the leaf into another bundle to be tied up; she works without looking down, her eyes saying, I, too, had to learn, and I, an outsider, had to step forward to become a part of this family.

Holding onto Isabel's hand, hearing the coquis and the bats flapping in the air, smelling the pasteles cooking, Magdalene knows this is a world that is not complete without every one of these family members, and it is a world that has room for the living and the dead.

Magdalene releases Isabel's hand, gives her a small nudge back toward Abuela. She turns away and stands on the edge of the portico. Little waves of pink streak the sky above the far mountains, bats swerving back and forth between pink and deep blue. There is a sudden wave of cool air and she hugs herself, rubbing her arms. The wave is gone and in its place she smells almonds, salt, the sea.

Last night she dreamt of a palm tree, and then, below a little white cloud floating above the tree, she saw a group who had taken to the sea in old boats, rafts strung together with inner tubes and plastic bags, nailed and secured with scraps of wood and cloth. Some wore hats. Some wore faded handkerchiefs—or what could have been old underwear, torn shirts. Many were bare chested, gleaming. A few had gallon containers of water. Some luckier ones had water and a few pieces of bread, some fried plantains, and strips of dried cod. Underneath a palm tree there was a mother on the beach, crying. She cried and cried, her body shaking as she waved good-bye to her sons, her only daughter. She shook so hard her feet sank into the sand. *I have no choice*, the mother wailed. *I am too old, but my children I will let go.*

The palm tree in Magdalene's dream shook violently. She found that the crying woman had now become her own mother, at first bitterly angry and yelling at Magdalene in an indecipherable language. But then her eyes turned puffy and red, and she saw tears shaped like almonds slowly falling from her mother's eyes into the sea. Her mother blinked, wiped her face, and then Magdalene saw herself standing on the beach, her feet twisted deeply in the sand. She was waving, yet she couldn't understand to whom or what. She couldn't tell if she was waving someone home or waving good-bye.

Magdalene thinks that she may need to make the same sacrifice. She, too, may need to let her daughter go. Her running may be over. Ernest had changed so much, he was becoming a man no one had imagined he would ever become. She felt and knew—she had no doubts—that Ernest was Isabel's father; deep within the vivid window of her memory of him, she felt his arms around her, heard the sound of waves, the sand warm and smoothly shaped from the motion of their bodies as they made love under a tree on the beach. Yet she was too afraid to tell him, too afraid to complicate or, worse, kill the life he had begun to dream and live. She could not bear the responsibility of barring his entrance into a new world beyond his past, some field he walked amidst a peace and grace he hardly ever knew.

She turns away from the night just as Isabel approaches, her hands and arms stretched in front of her, offering a plate with five pasteles. Ernest's mother walks behind Isabel, her hand on her back.

Mamí, for Ernestito. To give him in the mail.

Magdalene smiles, runs the tip of her index finger down Isabel's nose, who shrugs, goes up on her tiptoes, and laughs.

If you want, Ernest's mother tells her. We can freeze them and then send them.

Yes, that would be nice. Thank you.

Magdalene touches the top of Isabel's head, then raises her hand to Evelyn's shoulder.

Thank you, she says again, lightly squeezing her shoulder.

Ernest. His life, his story, has parts she has left behind, parts she has stolen. She sees a small cardboard box with black script around its sides floating high like a kite over the sea, a white string dangling from the box, Isabel holding on to the string and drifting farther and farther away, and then Ernest standing on the other side, his arms opened wide, waiting to embrace her.

The heron stood still in a pool of dark blue water. It raised one leg, curled up, river water falling softly, shattering its mirrored stillness, the heron's elegantly straight reflection. Isabel gasped, pointing. Magdalene held her back gently, her arm curved around her waist, Isabel ready to run for the river.

An outboard motor jumped to a start downstream, the whine loud over the tops of the birches. The heron lifted in a long span of gray and blue, the pool turning to waves. Magdalene could hear the heron's wings whirling around them, Isabel screaming as Magdalene let her go. Isabel twirled round and round, pointing, her face darkening in the shadows of the birches, Isabel trying to catch the last glimpse of the heron arcing out over the river. She turned back to Magdalene, stepped forward into a shaft of sunlight, the pine needles under her feet a dusty deep red. Isabel stood on one leg, the other curled back, heronlike, her arms lifted straight from her sides, her face almost still with amazement, her eyes wide open.

Magdalene waited.

Isabel slowly dropped her leg, and then she took off running, ready to lift up and fly.

Magdalene laughed, held her arm out as Isabel passed under. She turned around, Isabel swerving from the grove of birches, up the slight rise, and then disappearing.

She could smell the fish cooking, almost done, the sweet odor of hot grease and cornmeal. Plates clattered together, silverware tinkling. Magdalene turned west, away from the birch-tree shadows, which had become deeper, as if when the heron flew away she had left her blue imprint across the river-bank, in between the long white trees. She shivered, hugging herself. It had been such a beautiful, bright blue day. A last moment of Indian summer.

Isabel laughed, Juan growling after her echo.

Magdalene lifted her sweater from her shoulders, slid her arms through. She unpinned the yellow ribbon from the front of her sweater. She pulled her hair back and with one hand wrapped the ribbon around twice, then with both hands tied a small knot and a bow. She turned back to the river, the pool now calm. The wild rice and sorghum stalks silently swayed in the westerly breeze. The hem of her cotton dress breathed back and forth across her skin. This place, where Ernest had once lived, now so silent and still. A yellow leaf fluttered in the breeze, lightly, gently falling flat on the pool, scattering her face.

She heard her mother calling her name, calling her to dinner.

She walked up the rise away from the pool. The landscape had changed, had shifted with last year's spring flood. There had never been this rise of silt, and it almost covered the flat area of land where Ernest's cabin once stood. He had given her the land when he left, and Magdalene paid the small yearly taxes so they could have picnics and cookouts (and she often thought that one day Ernest might want to come back, maybe he'd want to live here again). One weekend, she and Juan and Isabel set up a pup tent. Only it was so warm—the night sky filled with the waving blacks and purples of the northern lights—they slept under the stars. With this winter's first snowfall she wanted to bring Isabel to look for animal prints, to see the snow against this river, and to take her sledding.

She stopped on the top of the rise, looking down on the flat, muddy square of dirt where the cabin had been. Ernest always walking out the door, two apple crates in his hand, his hair combed back, his lips twisting into a smile. He set the crates close to the river, where she stood now, where there had never been this silt. He'd show her how to put a crayfish on her hook and then how to throw out their lines. The sun setting. He lit a kerosene lamp, and they sat on the crates, holding hands, watching the river turn from gold brown to dark blue in the oncoming night.

Now there was only a small wall of brick left over from the foundation, a pile of rotting timbers. Some smashed beer bottles, an empty rum bottle. These could no longer be Ernest's. Now there could only be high school kids drinking on a Friday night. There was a small burnt circle from a bonfire.

Juan whistled.

Magdalene stepped ahead, down the rise.

Underneath the lone sycamore tree they all stood around the picnic table—her mother and stepfather, with napkins in hand; Isabel with half an ear of corn raised to her face, butter dripping onto her shoes; and Juan, with his back to her, his arm moving back and forth, the grease from the skillet on the grill crackling. He turned around, smiled weakly, a long bone-white platter piled high with fried bluegills. She walked forward and took the platter; his arms and hands shook in the air, and then he tucked his hands under his armpits. They looked at each other. Magdalene dropped her head, and when she turned to the picnic table with the platter of fish, she felt the edge of her sweater brush against Juan.

Her stepfather lifted Isabel to the table. She pointed at the top piece of fish. Magdalene set the platter down. Magdalene's mother lifted the top one for Isabel, then lifted a bluegill for each of their plates.

¡Mira! Isabel. The little bones, Juan said. He lifted the fish from his plate, lost in his hand, and took a bite. He chewed softly, cornmeal around his lips, then raised his fingers to his mouth and pulled out two small bones. He arched his eyebrows, smiled, wiping the grease from his lips.

Isabel giggled, waiting for Magdalene to spoon some potato salad onto her plate. Her mother and stepfather sat down.

Along with the fried fish and potato salad, they had a plate of deep red tomatoes sliced and salted; a tub of warm grilled corn; a bowl of onions and cucumbers creamed with buttermilk, vinegar, and crushed black pepper. The day had been almost too warm, almost seventy, and Magdalene put out a jar of tea to cook in the sun. Now it glistened with ice and lemon slices. For dessert Magdalene's mother had brought a carrot cake with cream frosting, the cake made fresh from fall carrots.

Magdalene sat down, across from Isabel.

Juan came to the table, handing Magdalene's stepfather, Mr. Swanson, a beer, another for himself in his hand.

Her stepfather led them in saying grace.

The sunlight reflecting off the water warmed the riverbank, brought heat to their table. They were noisy with their plates and spoons, the crunching of fish and cornmeal in their mouths. They spoke briefly of the weather, and of the beautiful colors beginning to appear in the trees. Juan, sitting next to Isabel, took a few bites from his fish. Mostly Juan drank from his beer, his eyes bloodshot and his face chalky save for the tips of his cheeks, bright red and dry under his eyes. His hand shook when he raised his spoon to Isabel's mouth. Magdalene wondered why he always seemed to look beyond her, as if he were living in another world. The more she looked at him, the more she could see he had been drinking more than eating.

A trio of ducks flew above the table, their shadows cutting across his face, flying to unknown places. Juan stood up, hiked his pants up to his waist, excused himself.

She watched him walk to the river, set his beer down, and then lift his fishing pole. He reeled the line in fast, checked the hook, a small, shriveled piece of pink meat on the end. He tore it off. He took a chicken liver from a plastic tub, slid it on the hook. He leaned back, flipped the pole, his light green line floating out into the current.

Magdalene's mother and stepfather stared at her with saddened looks, her mother perhaps more accusing, asking questions Magdalene couldn't answer.

Her mother raised her glass of iced tea to Isabel's greasy mouth. Then she wiped her face. Isabel chewed, her mouth open, happy with her food, the flavors in her mouth.

Instantly, Magdalene was happy, laughing inside.

Car tires squealed, from up above the hill, on Parkway Avenue. Car doors slammed. She looked at Juan, who turned and looked up the hill. Her mother and stepfather looked beyond her. Magdalene turned back. A man in a red tie ran by. A door to their car was open—an atlas flying out, cups, scraps of paper, Isabel's coat. Some children screamed off in the distance. The sound of metal hitting the sidewalk. Isabel started to cry, and just as Magdalene turned around to her, she saw the car door slam shut, the man in the tie ran by again, and then she heard the squealing of tires, their car gone.

Her mother held Isabel, crying, in her arms, her hand holding the back of her head. Her stepfather was standing, a blank, astonished look on his face. Magdalene stood up, her stepfather turning to Juan.

What happened? he asked.

Juan looked out on the river.

Magdalene walked from the picnic table toward him, but her stepfather put out his arm and held her back.

No, he whispered. Then to Juan:

Come on. What's going on? He pushed Magdalene back, harder.

What could he know? she wondered.

Isabel screamed louder, then her voice seemed to die. She could feel the muscles in her stepfather's arm tighten, his neck rigid, stiff. He yelled:

Listen, man. If you know, by God, tell us.

Juan jerked his arm back and threw his empty beer bottle into the river. He turned back to them, his face confused, embarrassed, a single tear rolling down his left cheek, his lips quivering. His hands shook and then closed to fists.

I haven't been working . . . I don't know . . .

He looked down at the ground, squatted on his heels.

I guess . . .

He stood abruptly, stared at Mr. Swanson.

I guess, I guess they repossessed the damn car.

He turned toward the river. He kicked the tub of livers, blood lifting into the air. He threw his tackle box into the river.

Juan, *no!* she screamed.

He grabbed his fishing pole and violently snapped it in half across his thigh, flinging the pieces into the river.

She went to grab him but Isabel cried out again. She turned to her, and then began to cry, confused, already seeing within her tears a time when she would return to this moment, how it changed the weather and beauty of this afternoon, the shame weighing heavy on Juan's shoulders, her own heart. And then to explain whatever it might steal from Isabel's memory.

She took Isabel from her mother's arms, holding her tightly. Over Isabel's shoulder she saw Juan off and running. She turned away, only to feel Isabel's head rise from her shoulder, and then Isabel calling out his name—*Juan, Juan*—his name echoing in her ears, and so she turned back once again, Juan disappearing into the warm October sun.

They walked home with the sun to their backs; Magdalene held Isabel's hand, the plate of tomatoes covered by cellophane in her other hand; her mother and stepfather walked alongside them carrying the rest of the leftovers. When they arrived, her stepfather wouldn't come inside, only kissed Isabel good night, then stood under the tree in the front yard waiting for her mother.

Magdalene put the leftovers away, closing the refrigerator door. When she turned around she said, Mamí, I had no way of knowing. He left every day for work, and it was like everything was . . .

I know, her mother said, bending down to hug Isabel and kiss her good night.

Magda, you can't just say, I thought everything was okay. First it was all that time with Ernest. God, I thought you might marry him and live down on the river in that . . . She stopped, closed her lips tightly and smoothed down the curls on the back of her neck.

Then it was Juan—what was going through your mind, mija?

Magdalene looked down on the floor, focusing on the little black specks in the white tiles, then heard again within her mother's words the deep, dark pain of memory:

You don't need to know your father. Where is he? Where did he go? Who cares! How many times have I told you? Puerto Rican men aren't worth shit.

Her mother stared at her, holding Isabel close. Isabel yawned, exhausted from the long walk, but for a moment, before her eyes closed, she looked up at Magdalene, her eyes appearing wide with sudden awareness.

Magdalene's mother told her:

None of this matters anymore. Now you have to talk to him, see the mistake you've made, think of what's best for Isabel. Do you really need him in your life?

She handed Isabel to her.

And right now you need to figure things out for yourself. There's no reason to get Ernest involved in any of this, you hear? Her mother left through the kitchen door, the screen door slamming twice and then quieting.

Now Magdalene sat at the kitchen table, their bankbook in front of her. After she had laid Isabel down on her bed, the child fell asleep without a fuss. Magdalene had changed from her cotton dress into a pair of shorts but still wore her sweater over a T-shirt in case of a chill. The river breeze blew through the open window above the sink, a last warm gust before winter. She loved this warm smell—apples, manure, fallen leaves, the wetness of the river. Leaves crinkled against the window, scraping the screen. Geese flew over the river, honking, their voices piercing the silence of the kitchen, the emptiness rattling inside her. Her hands opened, her arms extending. She opened the bankbook—angry with herself, shamed into anger for her irresponsibility, her inability to notice the signs. Juan's clothes never seemed to be that dirty, and they didn't always smell of burning paper and wood from the mill. He often came home late. In the morning she'd find him asleep on the couch, a small transistor radio playing next to his head. When she covered him with a blanket, Magdalene smelled the cigarettes and rum. She was too busy, working at school, grading papers, worrying over Isabel's first year in school; and so she thought he was working, took it for granted he was okay, maybe a little depressed, yet whenever she asked, Juan was unwilling to tell her what was wrong.

The last withdrawal, from a week ago, was for ninety dollars. There was only two hundred and twenty-six dollars left. The black stamped entries burned her eyes. She ruffled back through the pages. In June there was thirty one hundred dollars, then the withdrawals began. She let the pages close on themselves. There was no reason to try to trace the numbers, come up with some logic as to why the money had been taken. He had at least paid most of the bills, the rent. She pushed her chair from the table, stood up. She walked to the sink. Outside, the full harvest moon squeezed silver stripes of light through the trees, filling the empty backyard. She took an empty glass from the sink, turned the faucet on, the water warm and lifeless, running over the brim of the glass onto her hand, then shifting to cold. She lifted the glass to her lips, closing her eyes.

He must not have worked since early July, maybe sometime in June.

She set the glass upside down in the sink.

It had been such a beautiful day, and a breeze still came from the west, across the river, fresh, tinted with a warmth from places that seemed too far away.

She went back to the table and briefly thumbed through the bankbook, then tucked it behind the spice tins alongside the sink, her fingers brushing the tins, her nails ringing against them, the sound echoing in the bottom of the sink. The wet river came to her again, like some strong whisper from the past. She turned off the kitchen light, leaving the small light above the sink on. A moth pounced onto the screen, its vanilla wings crazy, instantly falling back into the darkness. She walked through the kitchen, stopped in the front room and lowered the lights. She could hear within the silence a greater silence: Isabel sound asleep, Juan not coming home tonight. She ran her arms along the walls in the darkness of the hall, and stepped through the door into the moonlight.

She walked swiftly across the street, then started to run when she hit the grass, her bare feet spongy and cool. She stopped on the edge of the Bond Street hill. The dam pounded on the rocks below, white mist rising to meet the light of the moon. The bricks of the paper mill were bright and smooth above the river, the silver water swiftly passing by. She stood next to a birch tree, its crisp leaves stirring in the breeze, and she put her arm around its trunk, needing its hardness to hold her up. Looking across the river, she saw how easy it was for the past to repeat itself, how small the world is. Smoke rose from the shore in front of where Ernest's cabin had been. A lantern hung from a tree. She saw a dark shadow move around the brightening bonfire. The leaves on the tree stirred, loud with a sudden burst of breeze. When it died she heard a scream. The bonfire sprung up, bright orange in the darkness, a lone figure sitting on its edge.

This is where he has been all the time. Right across the river. So close to us.

None of this matters anymore: Magdalene let her mother's words speak to her over and over again.

But it will always matter, she thought, *it has always mattered that you are filled with so much hate, Mamí, that you fill me with shame for painful memories I can't erase.*

In her mind she took her mother further to task: *Lorime, Mamí, do you remember him? Maybe hate like yours is what drove those men to beat him so badly.*

She let go of the tree, turned away from the river. She didn't want Isabel to awaken and find herself all alone. *Home. Isabel. It is all I have to run to.*

In early December Magdalene came home from work one day alone, Isabel spending the afternoon Christmas shopping with her mother. Juan had been gone for two nights, and then, on her way to work that morning, Magdalene saw him standing on the bridge. She stopped, leaned over, and rolled down the passenger's window. Juan came close, bending toward the window, shivering. He apologized, saying he'd gone fishing, had hitchhiked to Lake Michigan and back. *I needed something . . . but I don't know what*, he said. And then Juan promised he'd be home by the time she got home from work that evening.

The house was now silent, the sun weak behind the clouds, little patches of snow reflecting softly through the windows onto the living room floor. The lights on their Christmas tree throbbed red to green, green to blue, back to red. She had put the tree up early, trying to appease Isabel's constant questioning of when Santa was coming, and she also thought she might bring some cheer and life into the house.

She called his name. The kitchen was empty. The dish rack still full with the dishes she had done last night, and the bath towels she had washed that morning were still in a stack on the table, still feeling soft and fresh when she brushed her hand against them. She left the kitchen for their bedroom. He wasn't there. She slid out of her coat. She called his name again, laid her coat on the bed. She looked out the window into the backyard; the bare grass looked cold, wet, a faded winter yellow. The lone pine tree shook with wind. A robin crossed in front of her. She left the bedroom and went back to the kitchen to pick up the towels. She lifted them from the table, breathed in their flowery scent, then set them back down; she heard someone knocking at the front door.

Jeff Smith, a foreman at the paper mill, and Officer Graham stood on the small half circle of stone below the front steps.

Hi, Jeff—what're you doing here?

Can we come in?

Sure. But . . . It's not Isabel? she asked, her heart racing, her stomach filling with a wave of fear. She backed away from the door slightly, staring at Jeff.

No, it's not Isabel. Let's go inside.

She hadn't turned on any lights when she came home, and within the entryway they stood in a kind of grayish glow slightly brightened by the Christmas lights.

There's been an accident, Jeff said.

She looked at Officer Graham, his hat in his hands. He looked at her and in his eyes she could see who it was about. He asked, Maybe you'd like to sit down?

No, I'm fine. Please, what happened to Juan?

Well, I'm sorry to tell you, Magdalene, there's been, as I said, an accident, Jeff told her. A couple of hours ago, around one thirty, a worker noticed something floating below the spillway, off where we sometimes hold logs.

Juan, she said.

Jeff cleared his throat, his face turning redder.

Yes.

There was silence for a moment, and then the wooden floor creaked and popped from their collective weight. She wondered if Jeff and Officer Graham heard the same birds that she heard out front.

I'm very, very sorry, Maggie.

All she had wanted for this afternoon was to be alone with Juan. They had grown up together. Juan had never known his father, who had been killed in a bar, and soon afterward Juan lost his mother. They had a mutual past, memories to share, and at first it seemed so natural that they should live together. Yet she could never do anything for Juan's deep pain, nor could he for her longing, for her constant need to question who she was, where her life was headed, and the decisions she had made. She would finally admit to him this afternoon what he must've already known. *Juan*, she had rehearsed, *I still love Ernest.*

Again, I'm so sorry, Jeff said. We're not sure what happened. We're saying it *could've* been an accident, but we can't say for sure.

What do you mean?

Officer Graham stretched up on his feet, straightening his posture. He tucked his hat under his right arm and then tugged on his holster. Jeff cleared his throat again.

Well, Juan's been laid off since late May; he wasn't authorized to be on company property. He . . .

Magdalene interrupted Jeff. Yes, I know. He hasn't been working for some time, so there's no way to know how he ended up in the river.

Jeff's eyes widened, and then he said, Well, yes, I'm afraid so. That's right. We don't know why he was in our spillway.

He may have fallen . . . He may have jumped, she thought.

Officer Graham stepped forward, his hat in his hand again.

You have my deepest sympathies, Miss Swanson. We need a family member to officially identify his body . . . I realize there's no one in town. I've okayed it for you to do so. That is, if you're willing.

Officer Graham looked down at the floor. Jeff took a small step backward. The Christmas lights flecked their clothes with color, the sides of their faces red, green, then blue.

Magdalene blinked, the sound of the dam tumbling, pounding logs down below. When she was younger she often liked walking along the river, liked the productive, important sound of the shift horn bellowing, often watched the smokestacks blowing soot out across the river. The crashing of logs—a twenty-foot log rising out of the river and breaking in two when it slammed down against the rocks. A shroud of silver mist rising over her head. A figure dressed in green khaki work clothes floating in front of her, face down. She wondered how long he had been in the water, and she could only think how fragile Juan must have been smashed over and over again by those heavy logs.

Magdalene raised her hand to her hair, tried to run her fingers through it, and then stopped. She covered her ears, concentrating on the buzzing she found there. Then she said:

I will go. But could you give me just a minute?

66

Of course, Jeff answered. We'll wait right outside, and you take all the time you need.

Magdalene stepped back, stood in the small alcove of the living room, and watched the door close, the small click of the handle sharp, piercing. She turned away from the front door, went back to their bedroom to brush her hair—it felt tangled, thick—and to get her coat. There was a shaft of sunlight glinting on the bedroom floor and she watched it become a still, flat pool. She tasted her tears—on her lips, in the back of her throat. The fresh, clean scent of the towels came to her like summer rain, the wet river. Juan was dead. She wanted to call her mother. She wanted to tell her to please come quickly.

Mamí, I need you to come help me. My hair, it's tangled, thick, I've made such a mess.

Magdalene wiped her eyes, shrugged her coat on. She took the brush from her dresser and slipped it into her coat pocket. She stepped through the bedroom door into the hallway and closed the door behind her. And in this moment, sliding against the door to the floor, her head falling onto her knees, she suddenly thought of Ernest. She wondered where he was, what he was doing, what color shirt he was wearing, how he now combed his hair. She knew that she had made some mistakes, but she never meant for Juan to end his life.

We're saying it could've been an accident . . .

Magdalene looked through the archway, through the hall into the living room: red and green and blue lights blurring, the light of her tears colored, then fading to empty. She needed Ernest to fill this empty light. She needed Ernest to take her in his arms and help her stand up and, softly stroking her hair, whisper, *Ay, Magda, don't worry . . .* She needed to imagine that she and Ernest could walk in a field along the river and listen to the pounding dam as they came to terms with the death they were both a part of.

She stood up, pressing her back hard into the door. Down the hall, through the window in the front door, she could see Jeff and Officer Graham waiting. She walked toward them, her hand stretched out in front, ready to turn the handle.

With each morning that passes, Magdalene runs further away from death, her and Isabel's travels in foreignness less tentative, more particular. The barrio of Mocha becomes familiar and real because of the bird that always appears outside her window, because its whistle seems to repeat itself just for her. At first the bird seemed too unreal, a haunting meant to make the waking of each day all the more unbearable and lonely. But over these past three months this bird has become an intimate part of her life. To Magdalene, it now sounds almost human.

The sun hasn't risen yet, and there's only the faint light of dawn outside the window. Magdalene can hear Abuela in the kitchen, smell coffee on the stove. She turns over. Isabel stands next to her bed, her eyes wide open, excited, alive. As if there is no reason for sleep. She touches Magdalene's nose, then turns and runs from the room to Abuela. Magdalene lifts herself up, looks toward her table, her window.

The bird's whistle comes in a rhythm, a palpable pattern, in between the loud hisses and shrill screeches of other birds. Outside her window, across from the house, is a wide mound of red clay dirt. There's a twisted piece of steel driven into the ground. Nothing seems to want to grow on this patch of dirt, and it's only at the edges of the patch that life begins, a single mango tree on one side, and on the other, the never-ending cane fields.

Magdalene knows she'll never know the bird's song, but she takes that song and glues it within this new life that helps her to know the richness of such poverty. Ernest's abuelo had worked these cane fields for years, as did Ernest's father and Lillo: two generations giving their bodies and dreams for the riches the owner of this field has reaped. Saving any little bit of money he didn't have to spend, alongside his army pension, Abuelo had eventually bought a piece of land up the road on the mountain. The land was not a large parcel, but when he needed money to live he'd sell a small plot for someone to build a house. He gave a plot to Ernest's mother and father, perhaps as a gesture of apology or thanks for the childhood Ernest's father, Changó, had lost by working in the fields. The land on the mountain held some kind of forgiveness, and Changó and Lillo and Abuelo were building a house for Ernest's mother, Evelyn, as well as a small house for Abuela. Magdalene could see them eating dinner once Changó and Evelyn's house was complete, the table crowded with bowls and plates holding yuca, pasteles, breadfruit, gandules, yellow and orange mangoes, limes, and fat avocadoes—foods picked from their land. There's a silence between them as they eat, but the generations have been brought together—the mutual work finally coming to fruition, a solid tree filled with fruits and birds, blossoms and dreams.

Magdalene sits at her table. She has a stack of blue index cards to her right, and to her left, a collage a student had given to her as a gift when she finished her student teaching on Mackinac Island. In this room the window has no curtains; there are only hand-cranked metal blinds and a modern pair of outside shutters that can be closed and locked. In the windowsill a small goldfish bowl filled with clear marbles, their insides ribboned with orange, along with a few pieces of driftwood and sand-smoothed glass and stones from Lake Michigan. Magdalene prefers to leave the window wide open.

Yesterday, when Magdalene stood on the mound of red clay dirt, she turned away when Abuela found her. She looked deep into the cane and raised her hand to shield her eyes. Abuela laughed and took Magdalene's hand from her eyes and held it softly in her own. Abuela told her how she once found Ernest out here crying, and how that time became a story the family always shared whenever they thought of him. His father had been leaving for a barbacoa, and Abuela had told Changó that Ernest would stay home with her. Oh, Ernest wanted to go with his father, and he walked out here next to the mango tree and watched his father disappear into the field of cane. He cried and cried. He stood by the tree and watched the white ox chained to the piece of steel circling in the red-tinted dusk. Abuela came out to him, held his shoulder, and they stood together watching the ox fade away in the rising darkness. When they walked across the road to go inside and eat dinner, well, Ernest was no longer sad.

Magdalene tries to understand all that was behind the memories Ernest had shared with her. How could he always feel so alone? That last moment, at Juan's funeral, if only she had felt that he wanted her. He lifted his hands toward her, then dropped them to his sides, clasping them behind his back. He looked toward the ground. A silent cloud of time passed between them. Ernest looked up and said: Why don't you and Isabel come stay with me? He stood straight, rigid, and his words were confident, calm. His eyes were clear, and she wanted to believe that Ernest was sincere, that the lonely boy she had known was now standing there as a man on the other side of his past, his love openly offered to her. But for a moment she had a vague feeling of doubt; she wondered if he cared for her. And since he'd only just begun his new life, what gave her the right to change it? There was something about his posture, she remembers—the way he stood with a small bag slung over his shoulder, looking out across the rows of gravestones—that suggested he was still filled with loneliness, some form of tender apprehension.

She bends forward, her left arm on the table, and rests her forehead inside her palm. *He was still impoverished and striving for some wealth he needed to discover.*

Often what Magdalene remembers of Ernest is elliptical, terse, given without an exact sense of place. She remembers of herself that she never felt at home, never knew where she belonged—and hated herself sometimes for simply feeling, *I wish I knew my father.*

She never said yes or no to Ernest's offer; and he never brought it up again. She offered him a ride to town in the hearse. He declined, and after saying good-bye to Isabel, he left, walking away through the cemetery.

The morning is drifting away—the sun sparkles through the bowl, circles of light scattering across the face of the table. A little longer here and she'll then feel a greater need to go outside and be with Isabel and the family. She lifts the collage from the table. *Katie's*, she remembers. *A sailboat on a blue sea. Excel! Stay focused! A boy and a girl playing next to a sandcastle. We must lift up our hearts to be! A snow-covered windswept field.* There is a slim, cut-out picture of the John Hancock building, and next to that a glossy, idyllic image of the University of Chicago: students in T-shirts and shorts scattered about a wide quad of green grass, talking and reading books in soft golden sunlight, the tall doorway and spires of a church in the background. In maroon and gold letters Katie had pasted *Deserve Your Dreams!*

On the table there is also a stack of cream-colored envelopes from Ernest, and a recent picture of him—there are times when she can't help but look at him, yet the envelopes . . . She cannot bear to open them.

Magdalene needs to stay here a little longer and see Ernest's memories—see the shapes of her cutting, her pasting. She doesn't want to enter them with only his words, or her own memory of them. This is a dark region she must urgently enter, her hands turning the rudder in a swift current, her eyes scanning the horizon, searching the shore. Sailing out alone, Magdalene may discover her own memory of company, belonging, love . . .

And somewhere, my father . . .

She wants to learn from Abuela. She wants to see and feel the change from sadness to happiness that Abuela showed her, and she wants to see the white ox, the chain, the red clay dust powdering its hooves with every step. The hardness of this table, the reality of the never-ending cane fields outside her window, the sun the clock of her day—as time unfolds in the squared shadows growing on the edge of the portico, Magdalene's insides cry out, take shape in the air, float down the rows of cane. *No*, she says, *the shape of sunlight, fall leaves suddenly circling with wind and dust, a bucket of river water flung in the air.*

She will leave her window when the sun moves over the mango tree, the spaces between their fragmented memories becoming closer, as she creates the pieces and the glue for their lives.

Outside, the bird, the remnants of a rainbow, a storm rising over the mountains from the sea, the mound glinting with sun.

Isabel sits in the red clay dirt making dolls out of banana palms.

A hummingbird flutters above an orchid, its ochre throat bleeding into the flower's white.

The sun moves over the mango tree—a fruit's shadow bursting on the table. Like a little dark hand waving for her to come.

Come out, come outside.

Ernest had told Magdalene, Absolutely. I'll meet you on Mackinac Island the first weekend of August.

August was always a difficult time of year to find a place to stay, and especially the first weekend, when families traditionally came to the island; but luck was with Magdalene, and she found a private cottage on West Bluff. Each of the past four summers she had stayed in the same room in a boarding house, along with three other girls, a shower down the hall. This summer she roomed with three sophomores from Albion College, though they were no different than many of the other girls: they spent most of their time sunbathing, drinking, sleeping—and working just enough to pay for their drinking and to leave the island with a little more money than they had arrived with. Magdalene stayed away from the room as much as possible. Now she would have her own place when Ernest arrived.

The cottage was a little expensive but gorgeous. The inside bare and clean, the shiny wooden floors soaking up warm, honey gold sunlight. There was a four-poster double bed, a lamp on either side of the bed, a leather club chair with a footstool, and a small bathroom with a sink and a claw-foot tub; outside, around the back of the cottage, there was a shower with a pull-chain handle and a birch pallet to stand on. The cottage didn't have a kitchen, but yesterday Magdalene had brought up an electric percolator, a can of ground espresso, and two coffee cups. There's plenty of light here, she thought, taking in the skylight and four windows; one set of windows looking out on the woods to the northwest, while another set looked out on a small sloping field to the southwest, where the field disappeared into the deep blue freshwater sea: Lake Michigan accentuated by the Mackinac Bridge arching over, the woods to the northwest crowding out the horizon. A few watercolors of boats and lighthouses hung on the wall. There was a desk and a chair in front of the windows facing the lake.

Magdalene turned to the desk. She decided this was for Ernest. In the right-hand corner of the desk, under the windowsill, she placed three books she had brought with her: Conrad's *Lord Jim*, Neruda's *Passions and Impressions*, and the old copy of Lardner's stories she had given to Ernest many years before. She placed a pencil and pen in front of the books, along with a stack of blue three-by-five cards, the thick and soft kind made with cotton. Against a short water glass she propped up her favorite postcard: a copy of Manuel Álvarez Bravo's *Que chiquito es el mundo, 1942*.

Unfolding the small wooden table she had brought from her room in town, Magdalene stood in front of the northwest windows and set it down, and then pushed a chair up to its edge. She wanted the setting to be perfect: *We can both look through our windows, on the same side of the cottage, both of us looking out on the field, the sailboats and ferries, the curling white waves.*

Everything is ready, she thought; now I only wait for his arrival.

Magdalene rode her bike back along the lake on her way to the library in town. A ferry was approaching from the mainland, a huge tail of water spraying from behind it, another ferry on its way back curving around the arriving ferry's wake. The sun felt bright and warm, even with a cold breeze pushing in from the northwest. The azure water sparkled with sunlight, and when the breeze paused, Magdalene heard waves crashing on the stony beach to her right. Up above her, on West Bluff, the Grand Hotel's verandah: the white chairs filled with guests, the West Indian servers quickly crossing the verandah in their black bow ties and white jackets, glinting ice-filled drinks perfectly balanced on trays. The road to town was packed with bikes, mostly families of four or six beginning trips around the island, slowly peddling by, looking up at the school, the hotel, the horse-drawn carriages clomping down the road, the lake, the bridge in the distance. She turned into the library, parked her bike by the side, and locked the back tire to the frame.

The library had been built on the lake, and on clear mornings the sun rose bright and warm in the back bay windows. The library looked like an elegant white lake cottage trimmed in robin's-egg blue. Magdalene often thought it was one of the most beautifully designed structures on the island, not just for the way it looked, but simply because it was a library—that quiet space where anyone could find something compelling to read. She worked at the circulation desk, helping as well with an occasional reference request.

Magdalene stepped inside. Mr. and Mrs. Morris were sitting at a large table reading the *Detroit Free Press*; Mrs. Morris looked up and winked, pushing her glasses back on the bridge of her nose. Mary Doyle, the head librarian, was bent over a bunch of boxes; she pulled out certain volumes, looked them over carefully, and then placed them into certain stacks or boxes. Tomorrow the library was having its annual book sale. Magdalene slipped off her sweater, hung it on the back of a chair, and joined Mary sorting the books.

Isn't your beau coming in today? Mary asked.

Technically, he's not my boyfriend, she told her. He's just an old friend I grew up with.

Hmmm. Ernest, you said, right?

Yes. Ernest.

Nice name. Mary lifted two volumes in one hand, looked down their spines. She put one book back in the box, the other in a stack she had started on the table to her right.

I'm putting nineteenth-century fiction in this stack, which we have plenty of, and twentieth-century fiction in this stack. Any kind of history I'm leaving in this box. Mary had written *History* with a red marker on its side.

What can I do?

Maybe you can start an essay section for us—that's always a big draw.

Sure. Magdalene immediately spotted a paperback edition of Emerson's essays, pulled it out of the box, and placed it on the table. She tore a flap off the box and with the red marker wrote *Essays*. She placed the flap in front of the Emerson.

Mary said, It just seems to me, considering all you've done to prepare for his visit, this Ernest must have been, or you wish him to be, your boyfriend.

Now, Mary, I already told you . . .

I know, I know . . . She blew the dust from the cover of a book, placed it on the nonfiction stack.

How's the cottage?

It's great, gorgeous. Thanks for talking to the owners and recommending me, Mary.

You're welcome. Glad it's all working out. Can you hold down the fort for a bit?

They looked around. Mr. and Mrs. Morris had gotten up. They waved— We'll see you tomorrow, Mrs. Morris said—and then they stepped outside. The library was empty. Magdalene smiled at Mary.

Sure.

Mary took a few awkward steps around the boxes and then found a pathway straight through, adjusting her long skirt and stepping into a bright shaft of light falling from the skylight. Magdalene blinked, and when she looked up Mary was almost to the door. She stopped, turned around.

Oh, before I forget: behind the counter you'll find a small shopping bag for you.

Magdalene stared at her for a moment, shook her head with understanding.

Thanks.

No problema, kid. You and your *old friend* have a good time. She wiggled her nose and added, Don't do anything I wouldn't do.

Mary held two fingers up and waved a peace sign at her. Magdalene picked up a book and bluffed as if she were ready to throw it. Mary waved her peace sign more quickly, opened the door, and stepped outside. Magdalene turned toward the back of the library, toward the bay windows. A window shuddered with the breeze; seagulls screamed in the harbor; a *ring-ring* from a bike's bell; and the clean sound of the breeze, her breathing. Beginning to sort the books again, her eyes latched onto a faded red *Webster's Dictionary*, the spine cracked, the pages brittle, yellow, and smelling of brewer's yeast. The word *become* jumped out at her: *to come, change, or grow to be; to befit; suit*. Her fingertips began to itch from the book's oldness. When she lifted her left hand from the page, Magdalene noticed the small spots her fingertips had left on the page, and then directly across from *become* she saw the word *beau: a girl or woman's sweetheart*.

She looked up from the dictionary. White waves crashed in a froth onto the stony shore. The lone birch tree bent in the breeze, the silver undersides of the leaves glinting with the twisting waves. The sky was bright blue, a few puffy clouds floating slowly overhead.

Can a girl's friend become her sweetheart? She wondered why she had asked Ernest to visit. Why hadn't she thought of this before . . . ? *Only to see him . . . to see who he has become.*

A ferry banked to the left in front of the library, making a wide sweeping turn into the harbor, a flock of seagulls circling above the ferry's spray.

And for Ernest to see me . . .

She hadn't seen Ernest in over six years. The first year she went away to college, never coming home during the fall or Christmas breaks, she tried to fill her mind with her studies, tried to immerse herself in a different life. But deep down she felt that she was afraid to change. She wondered who she might become, and it scared her to think she might move too far away from her past. There were so many things her mother had never told her—who she was, her past, her life, Magda's past.

Mamí, who's my father?

She never answered.

Maybe that had been the reason why Magdalene wasn't sure, at first, if she should go away to college. But she did go, and her first year she had to study hard and stay away from home to forget the violent argument she had had with her mother when she suggested she might not go.

Who am I, Mamí? What gives me the right to go away and become the person you dream of? I don't even know where I come from.

She sometimes still felt the force of her mother's hand when she punched Magdalene in the throat, pulling hard on her hair.

You won't stay here; you won't live in my house. Please, don't ruin your life . . . Magda, please, not for Ernest, not for a Puerto Rican. You don't have to be a disgrace; you can become and have so much more than I ever did.

It had all become one conversation for Magdalene, though there were many more, and even though her mother never hit her again, each time they spoke her hands were clenched with rage, sometimes shook at her side, and Magdalene fell back into herself waiting for the hard anger of her mother's hand. Her mother was powerful; she was never a disgrace. She was simply bitter, lonely, afraid to share whatever it was that filled her with so much hate—and it was powerful, strong, muy fuerte. Magdalene knew she had to go away to college after they had fought. To become, to understand her past, Magdalene felt she would first have to leave her mother's hatred behind; she'd need to find another strength.

She tried to send Ernest a few notes and cards that first year away at school, but she was never sure he had ever received them, and, if he had, he never returned in kind. That summer she did go home. She went to visit Ernest but found his cabin empty. There was a neat pile of wood near the door; yet she could tell there had been no fires for a long time. She didn't see Ernest's fish trap; the hard dirt from his walking back and forth in front of the cabin, standing and throwing the trap out into the currents, had been replaced by fresh green grass. There was no sign of the chain that had held the trap to the ground. She stepped up to the cabin door, and inside she found his bare cot, and on top of it, in a plastic sandwich bag, Ring Lardner's *Haircut and Other Stories*. She took it from the bag, turned the cover.

> Dear Magdalene,
> I didn't want your gift to go to ruin. Please keep it for me.
> All my Best,
> E.

Magdalene closed the cover, sensing a shadow behind her as the cabin became darker. She remembered that Ernest had asked of her the same when they were fifteen-years-old, and he had gone away to work with the men in the fields. She turned to the shadow. Her stepfather stood on the other side of the doorway, his arms open. She closed the cabin door, the book in her hand. Her stepfather held her and told Magdalene he was happy to have her home. Ernest had moved away in the spring, he said. One day he came to him, out of the blue, all clean and dressed up in a dark maroon sweater and a pair of khakis. He hated to ask, and he knew he had no right to do so, but he wondered if he could borrow two hundred dollars. He told Magdalene's stepfather he was leaving and would pay him back soon. Two weeks later Ernest sent her stepfather a money order from South Bend for two hundred and twenty-five dollars, and in the envelope he included a deed for the cabin, notarized, in Magdalene's name. Her stepfather held her tighter, told her not to cry, and then he let go of her and asked her not to worry; Ernest was doing okay. He had a friend who was the foreman at an Old Gold tomato-canning plant outside New Carlisle; he learned from him that Ernest had worked as a laborer, laying down irrigation pipes in the celery, asparagus, and pickle fields; that he was a good worker, had worked for a few months at the cannery, too; but then he took a job at another plant in South Bend.

That same summer Magdalene saw Juan; he was sitting on an old apple crate fishing in front of Ernest's cabin on a Saturday afternoon. Juan was working at the paper mill, and they talked about going to find Ernest, to see how he was doing, say hello. They would meet on Saturdays at the cabin, but they were never sure where they should start looking for Ernest, and Juan worked long hours at the mill and never seemed to have the time. They eventually never spoke of it again, and if they had some time together on the weekends they often went up to St. Joe, down below the bluff, and swam and sunbathed without even talking about Ernest. But it was like he was there, silent, lying between them in the sand, rising with the waves.

For the last four summers Magdalene had worked up here on the island; making fudge, working on a ferry, waiting on tables in restaurants and pubs, working in this library. She never went home again for the summer. She had finished her undergraduate degree. Next spring her master's in education would be complete, and a guaranteed job with the Niles School System awaited her. Next month, in September, Magdalene would student teach here on the island, right across the street from this library, and then in the spring she would return to complete her final semester of classes.

Now Magdalene placed two more books in the nineteenth-century pile.

This past Christmas she went back home to visit her parents. She took a girlfriend, Jean; she couldn't bear to face her mother alone. When she asked Jean to come along, she pulled two tickets from her back pocket, and she promised her the trip wouldn't be all small town, and so one day they took the Amtrak to Chicago to do some shopping. It was one of those splendid, fortunate, warm December days; it hadn't snowed yet, and the wind wasn't too strong. They spent most of the morning and the early afternoon shopping in the Water Tower. Jean's hands were heavy with bags, some Christmas presents she wanted to send home. Magdalene picked out a light gray cardigan for her stepfather and a small tub of Italian bath salts and a silver brush with delicate, soft hairs for her mother. Magdalene and Jean could see how bright it was outside and wanted to get out on the streets.

They turned east and made their way to Lakeshore Drive and looked at the Mies van der Rohe building. The open, cubed lobby was filled with high light, the lake to the east and south blue and silver through the glass.

They turned north and followed the sidewalk past the older residences, the trees lining the street black and bare, yet warm and not so empty in the winter light they walked in. They passed the Drake Hotel and then crossed onto Oak Street. Windows held fancy designer clothes—oddly cut, brightly colored fabrics, expensive watches and pieces of jewelry. Shoe boutiques and galleries shared the same entrance. Oak Street was full of people, shopping bags swinging at their sides. They made their way into a quiet residential area, a mixture of older buildings and new construction. There was a small park; across from it Magdalene could see the Newberry Library. They walked the small paths, watching women not much older than themselves pushing strollers, their children thickly bundled in fleece and wool.

There was a coffee shop on the corner, its window filled with mist and warmth, the afternoon air beginning to chill. They could see flaky, buttery croissants stuffed with tomatoes and brie on white plates inside a brightly lit case, the strong bite of coffee in the air. They went inside. Magdalene raised her hands to warm them, her bag caught in the crook of her elbow, and as soon as she dropped her hands to her sides she found herself staring at a boy she thought she'd never see again: now he wasn't a boy at all; he was a young man. He immediately stood up with recognition, putting his pen in the spine of his book.

Ernest stood in front of her in a black suit, without a tie, his hands tucked under his armpits as if he were hugging himself.

Hello, Magdalene.

He let his hands fall to his sides, suddenly clear that he was seeing her and that she recognized him. They hugged warmly yet with years of distance between them. They couldn't stop repeating how shocked they were to see each other. Magdalene introduced Ernest to Jean. He said hello, shook her hand, looked down at his table, books and papers spread about, then started to bring them into some kind of order. She stopped him, her hand on his shoulder, his body firm, warm. She told him: We're just getting coffee to go, Ernest. We have to catch a train. He said, Sure, sat back down. She felt his eyes on her as they ordered. When Magdalene turned to say good-bye he held her arm for a moment. He bent over his table, lifted a folded piece of paper to his lips, and then swiftly wrapped an orange and red scarf around his neck. He took the paper from his lips.

I tried to reach you, several times. And I left different addresses with your mother.

They looked at each other knowingly.

I guess she never let you know.

He opened the door for them.

Outside, the sun was to the west behind the Loop, the tall buildings leaving cold gray shadows broken at times by small strips of sunlight. Several cars honked in succession. It began to snow lightly, fat flakes falling all around them, landing wet on Magdalene's cheeks, her eyelashes. Ernest stood on the corner, cars rushing past, his hand held high, his scarf blowing in the wind. A cab stopped. He opened the back door, said something to the driver, handing him some money. He said good-bye to Jean, held her bags as she scooted inside with her coffee, and then he handed them to her.

Magdalene walked up to the cab. He leaned against the open door, stood in front of her, and raised his hands to her cheeks. They trembled for a moment and then steadied when he held her face. He whispered into Magdalene's ear:

Just let me know how you are, Magda, when you get a chance, especially now since you know where to find me.

He let go of her face, firmly slipped the piece of paper inside her coat pocket.

Good-bye.

Bye. Merry Christmas, Ernest.

Merry Christmas to you, too.

He closed the door, his open hand on the window for a moment, the deep lines and crosshatches on his palm imprinting themselves in Magdalene's mind, her face burning.

A book fell apart in her hands, the spine cracking in half as soon as she opened it. Magdalene dropped it into a box holding other torn, water-damaged, broken books to be taken outside and given away. Lifting an empty box, Magdalene held it against her thigh, stuck her finger in the seam on the bottom and broke the box down. The sun caught in her eyes; it had shifted to the northwest, beginning its descent. She heard the handle on the front door click. Mary stepped inside.

It's four fifty, Magdalene; we might as well call it a day.

Mary walked toward her with a cup of coffee in her hand. She looked at Magdalene oddly.

What's a matter with you, girl? I never seen such a red face; you look like you've been running for hours.

She set the coffee down. She touched Magdalene's cheeks, and then took her in her arms.

I've never seen such a thing. Four summers in a row up here—no family, no old friends . . . She stroked the back of Magdalene's head, her hair, gave her a hard squeeze. She held her at arm's length, tucked a strand of hair behind Magdalene's left ear.

You've got so far to go, Magda. No matter what someone hasn't shared with you, no matter what seems lost . . . The world doesn't have to be so lonely—and it doesn't always have to *work*. Remember how small it is, how there's always someone. Right now, you and I are together.

Magdalene felt tears rolling down her cheeks and she let them fall, but she did not want to cry out loud. For the first time in a long time she felt how much she longed to be around someone else, how she no longer wanted to run away or become someone else. *For six years I've never given of myself freely to anyone*, she thought, *my life closed off from the company of others as I searched beyond my past, my mother's hate.* She told herself, *Stop searching. You've searched for so long that that's the only thing you've discovered: running, empty fields, running.*

She felt the imprint of Ernest's hand on her in the cab that day. The rust brown of a steel bridge finally cut through the window, and she saw the dark olive green river passing by. Stop, she yelled, stop. She turned to Jean: I'll be right back, Jean, right back. Just wait here.

Magdalene jumped out of the cab and ran back across the bridge, the evening wind like a knife cutting her face. She stopped in the middle of the bridge, her lungs aching with icy air, her face raw and alive, her eyes watery and blurry. She wiped them, the Wrigley Building tall in the falling snow. She followed the Chicago River east, winding its way between skyscrapers, underneath bridges, the river and the snow becoming a string of music she listened to and followed into the distance—a small patch of blue, the freshwater sea she could never be that far from: Lake Michigan. Ernest had seen and recognized her immediately—*why?* she wondered. How did he know it was her? *He still does—he has always cared.*

She reached in her coat pocket and pulled out her yellow hair ribbon. She had worn one when she was young, but ever since Ernest had tied her hair with the ribbon, she kept a yellow ribbon close at hand.

She lifted her hand in the cold wind, let the ribbon stream and snap above the river.

She saw a fall day on the river, standing on the bank in front of Ernest's cabin, both of them dripping wet from the river, standing in their underwear, Ernest holding her yellow ribbon. Her face clean and wet and brown—that's what he saw; and her almond eyes, and how her long hair curled even more from the wetness of the river. Her hair was now a little longer, just to the ends of her shoulder blades, and a little darker; almost all mocha brown since the summer's lightness had faded away in the fall. But he recognized her and stood up. She had probably been standing in the coffee shop straight as a board, her arms across her chest, her open hands gripping her biceps, looking at the menu on the wall with confidence and meaning—*leave me alone*, her posture said, and yet Ernest had known it was her.

She let go of the ribbon, watched the yellow spin above the river, pick up lightness and speed as it crazily twisted and tumbled through the air. It hit the river. No matter how hard she looked the ribbon seemed to instantly disappear. She let it go, starting quickly for the cab. She let it go for Ernest: he always lived close to water, and here in this big city, between the river and the sea, their yellow ribbon could help bring them together.

Mary took the lid off the coffee and handed it to her.

I no longer want to run. I am me, here, Magdalene told herself.

The harbor, the lake, the light behind the library was becoming deeper, darker, a cool blue shadow against the white walls. She took a sip from the coffee, let its bitter warmth swirl around the back of her teeth, slowly draining down her throat. *I want a shadow as cool as the blue to envelop me.*

You're okay, right?

Yes, fine. I thought of something . . . Well, I've been thinking too much. I don't know what happened. But nothing will ruin this weekend.

Good, Mary said, shaking her fist triumphantly in the air.

It looks like it's going to be a beautiful weekend, Mary.

I think so. Now you take your time in the morning, but if you can come in around ten for a bit, that'd be great.

I will. I better get going, though; I need to get down to the dock.

You go on, I'll see you tomorrow.

Magdalene walked behind the counter and picked up the shopping bag Mary had for her; she looked inside and found a bottle of wine and two glasses. She slipped her sweater on. She walked about halfway across the main room and stopped. She held the bag next to her face and gave it a little shake.

Thanks again, Mary. See you later. She took another sip of the coffee.

You know, Mary, you may be right; I may have a beau.

Magdalene could hear Mary laughing as she stepped outside.

When Ernest walked off the ferry Magdalene recognized him easily; he was the only person in a suit. He had a red gym bag slung over his shoulder, a tartan plaid throw rolled under his arm, and he held a crisp white paper bag with string handles. Porters rushed by in the space between them, carrying luggage to bikes and rolling bikes out onto the road. The crowd was loud and excited: people yelling directions, trying to find bags and bikes, deciding where they'd go first. Magdalene lifted her arm high and waved. Ernest looked up, smiled, and waved back.

You made it.

Of course; the first weekend of August, just like I promised. Ernest opened his arms and they hugged awkwardly, his bag coming between them, and with Magdalene's bike against her leg.

It's good to see you, he told her.

I'm glad you came.

Ernest took her bike and handed her the grocery bag. She smelled lemon, seafood. Ernest raised his eyebrows.

Have you eaten?

No, I was waiting for you. Magdalene pointed to the bag in her front basket, the loaf of bread and cheese and tomatoes she had picked up, and the wine Mary had given them.

Which way? Ernest asked.

Magdalene swept her arm to the left, and they moved away from the dock through the crowds spilling out of the fudge shops and ice cream parlors. Bikes sped past, turning into the northwest curve of the road, past the Lakefront Hotel. A carriage driver smacked the haunches of a horse, the horse jerking the carriage forward, the driver snapping the reins faster.

I've always wanted to see this place, Magdalene; it has been nice to think of you up here for the last four summers. And it was wonderful riding over, looking out and seeing the outline of the town and then being aware of the exact moment when all the white and yellow houses become distinct. *Amazing.* Ernest raised his head, pointing his chin down the road, up to the bluff and the old fort, the brightly painted Victorians below.

I've become attached to it; it will be hard to leave. There are people who come up here every year, every August. A bike's bell rang behind them—*on your right, on your right*—and they stepped over to the side, a long line of bikes pedaling by. Magdalene leaned into Ernest, nudged his ribs, and pointed.

That's the library, where I work.

In front of them was a perfect view: the bridge in the distance, the evening sky a light blue filled with streaks of orange and pink, the freshwater sea a deepening blue in the waning sun. Ernest had his arm around her shoulder, and when she turned and smiled in that small instant of pleasure from looking out onto the water, the bridge seeming suspended in midair, Ernest kissed her lightly on the lips. She looked into his brown eyes, the breeze lifting his wavy brown hair, put her arms around him, closed her eyes and kissed him hard, breathed in deeply the smell of his hair, his skin, tasted his tongue.

She led him off the road, up a small incline.

Leave the bike here; I want to show you something. They dropped the bags next to the bike, and she took his hand and they walked up to the schoolhouse.

This is where I'll teach this fall—in just two more weeks we'll begin. They walked closer, up to the window of her room. Ernest shaded his eyes with his hands, pressed his face close to the glass.

Magdalene had pushed her desk to the side of the room, rearranged the students' desks in a half circle facing the blackboard. Across the length of the blackboard were twelve twenty-four—by—twenty-four-inch pieces of white construction paper, and Magdalene had written in the middle of each one a big, green question mark.

Ernest leaned back against the window, taking her hands.

What are the white squares for? He pulled her close to him.

I have twelve students, and so on the first day we'll talk about what a collage is; they'll probably know, but I've got some examples by Picasso to show them, and then we'll read a few stories from *Aesop's Fables*, and I want to suggest that he's repeating situations, like-minded characters, words—almost like he's drawing from the same place and cutting and pasting similar things into some of the fables. That night I want them to create a collage—from newspapers, magazines, labels, postcards, and old mementos—that they feel best describes their lives.

He pulled her a little closer, their hips touching. The smooth wool of his pants was soft against her bare legs.

Their collages will have to fit on one of the white squares, covering up the question mark. I'll leave them up all fall so we can always remember the worlds we come from. And we'll use them to help us talk about language, reading, how it is we each make meaning.

Ernest rubbed her arm with the back of his hand. It sounds excellent.

After Magdalene had seen Ernest in Chicago that past Christmas, there were weeks she couldn't stop thinking about him, wondering what he was doing, why it was so odd and simple that they had run into each other. She wanted to write to him right away; she felt too awkward and self-conscious at first, and then she became afraid of what she might say, right or wrong, how it may have been best that they went away from each other; and when she heard her mother's voice again, *How many times have I told you Puerto Rican men aren't worth shit*, she wondered if maybe there wasn't some deep harmony of resolve working to keep them apart. She spent the rest of the winter edgy, filled with a vague anxiety she couldn't come to terms with. A friend recommended brandy for her stomach, to help her sleep. All day she read and prepared early to take her exams, pack what she needed for the summer, and head up to Mackinac. Around eleven at night, she'd fill a small glass with ice cubes and brandy, the liquor too hot without ice. Reading under a lamp, sipping the brandy, her stomach became less and less tense, and about the time she finished her second glass, she could barely keep her eyes open, and she then slept like a baby. It had helped for a bit, but then the anxiety came back; in her mind she'd see Ernest sitting at that table, books and papers all around, smell the rich, freshly brewed coffee, and she'd suddenly feel afraid, unsure of her life, saddened about how time unfolded in such a way as to betray her deepest desires: *Why couldn't the Ernest I saw in Chicago have been my friend these last few years? Why were so many years filled with such loneliness? And of all the times I wished to see him, why didn't he ever appear then?*

One day in early March the weather in Ann Arbor became balmy; she was out walking through campus in a pair of shorts, a sweater. She sat down on a bench outside the law school, the sun warm on her legs, looking at the stained-glass windows and the ornate archways leading into corridors. She took a few blue index cards from a stack she had in her sweater pocket, and she began to describe the green of the stained glass, the sounds of the birds, the way the light seemed to cut certain archways in half, and then, *I wish you could see this, Ernest* appeared from her hand. She continued to write to him, tell him what she was up to, wonder what he was doing, how things were in Chicago, and then she closed with an ending she especially liked, from van Gogh: *I've filled up my paper, so I shall end and go out for a walk.* She walked to the post office, bought an envelope and a stamp, and mailed the index cards to Ernest. He wrote back. They continued writing to each other, every week or so, and then in May, right before she left campus, she called and asked if he'd meet her here the first weekend of August.

She hugged Ernest tightly, held him close for a bit. She whispered: Ernest. I know I don't know who you are. In all the letters you sent this spring, I could sense you are no longer who I remember. But I can live with more than my memory, and I want you to know how much I've missed you.

I've missed you too, Magdalene.

She took his hand and walked back down the incline. She grabbed her bike, and Ernest took up the bags and the throw. They walked to a small hill shaded by two tall birch trees. Magdalene locked her bike to the thinnest tree, and then she helped Ernest spread out the throw. He took off his coat, folded it, and laid it on the edge of the throw. He slipped off his shoes, pulled off his socks, and rolled them into a ball. Magdalene kicked off her sandals, and they sat down. Ernest took out two paper plates from his bag.

I bought these in Mackinaw City, just before I boarded the ferry. Ernest opened the white box, placed a fried soft-shell crab on Magdalene's plate, one onto his own. He had cut-in-half lemons, a bottle of hot sauce. There were two bags of salt-'n-vinegar chips, two brownies dusted with powdered sugar. He took out napkins and plastic forks, a small folding knife.

This is from my boss, my friend Mary. She handed him the bottle of red wine and a corkscrew. He looked at the label, held the bottle up to the beginning of the evening's light. He began to open it. Magdalene broke the bread into pieces, slicing two pieces in half. She placed slices of brie on the bread, added tomatoes. She took out the wineglasses. Ernest poured and they raised their glasses.

To the good life—as humble, gratifying, and easy as this very moment, he said, his glass raised high.

They clinked their glasses, drank. The crabs were juicy, crunchy, and full of flavor—black pepper, mustard seed, garlic, buttery flour, lemon. Their mouths crunched with batter and shell. The light lingered on the edge of the horizon. They watched the white sailboats gliding on the short, silvery white waves, ferries speeding quickly past the outer buoys, the outline of Bois Blanc Island becoming more and more definite, the small lights on the bridge brightening in the twilight; and on the road, couples strolling by hand in hand, groups of bikes passing, a young man with his arm around a young woman who pushed a stroller, two little legs kicking in the air.

Ernest spoke so easily and dreamily; one more year to go and he'd have his master's, and if he worked hard for three or four more years he could earn his PhD. For Ernest it was all dream: working at the small bookstore, going to classes, writing papers, spending long hours in the Newberry Library, and whenever things became strange and unreal and he began to doubt how he ever left behind his past to imagine this life, Ernest walked east past the outer drive and sat on the breakwater and stared at the freshwater sea.

What's most scary, Magdalene, is how many days I go without being around anyone I really know.

It was turning darker now. Small bonfires appeared on the beach. A light on the outer buoy began to spin around, a path of white cutting through the water.

It is such a strange feeling—it's almost like I'm no one, and yet I'm so aware of how much I like living in Chicago, walking the streets, staying up late in a coffee shop with a book, going to sleep with my mind . . . Well, there's only one way to say it—my mind ravished by language, sounds and smells, images, the certain gestures of people. But how can I ever express who I am, who I'm becoming?

She would never forget his face in the darkening twilight, the sky light blue from the stars, the rising moon. She couldn't answer him. She saw park benches, pigeons, trees beginning to bud; remembered Ernest describing the importance of his long walks, his afternoons to see and be, as he often wrote in his letters.

His eyes were filled with tears; he leaned back, closed them, and took a sip of wine.

I miss Lorime, some days . . . Any of us in that town could have been beaten; for our names, something about the color of our skin, our eyes, maybe because our hair isn't thin or straight. Who knows? But he was the one who was beaten. Who knows, there's so much that continues on unfinished . . .

I know, Ernest, she told him. But we are here and we can tell it to each other.

Ernest took another sip, ran his hand through his hair, squinted. He said, I miss him . . . or then, I guess, some days I suddenly realize I haven't missed him, or my father and mother, and then I'm filled with a kind of shame that may last for days.

Magdalene broke off a little piece of cheese from her bread, raised it to her lips, and then put it back on the plate without taking a bite.

Ernest said, But there's something else.

Go ahead, Ernest.

Lorime was one of my best friends. We spent whole summers together— Lorime, Juan, and me—fishing, playing baseball, swimming. When my father brought me back from Puerto Rico, I was so happy they lived in Niles, and you, too, Magdalene.

He lifted his feet in the air, stretched his toes, and then crossed his legs at the ankle. He wedged his wineglass in the space between his legs, grabbed his knees, and rocked back and forth for a moment.

But maybe all that was accidental. I mean, we knew each other and were friends because we were—us four—the only Puerto Rican kids in that town. It was horrible how Lorime died; I'll never forget that, and in not forgetting I'm trying to learn what I can and what I cannot control. I can't tell, though, if this is just a waste of energy, or a part of me I'll always need to face.

She said, I think I know how you feel. In my worst moments, when I just stare at my books, can barely write down two or three words, I'm filled with this ugly, sore feeling in my stomach . . . fear, I think. I thought it had to do with living alone for a few years, feeling then how much I missed my mother's house. And the lingering wondering about my father. I would tell myself, Maybe if I ask Mamí in a certain way, if I look in the right place, I might find him. You know what?

Tell me.

Please, give me some more wine, first. Ernest filled her glass. They each took a swallow.

I used to have this weird way of imagining your father's life, seeing you living on the river all by yourself: excitement, challenge, filled with romance is how I imagined it. I mean, God, the stories you shared with me, the memories—how could I not find that life persuasive. This one Saturday in August was unbearable; it was almost a hundred and the humidity was thick, no clouds in sight, plenty of sunshine. You know, one of those southwestern Michigan August days. None of us slept the night before, and my parents decided to go up to St. Joe for the day, to swim, to see if being by the lake might help us get away from the heat. All the way up, once we left Niles, we continued to see signs for Vollman's Market—peaches, apricots, potatoes, chilled watermelons. We were already burning up, in need of something cold, and I think we all wanted to stop just to get out of the car for a minute. But then I noticed my stepfather quit reading the signs, stared straight ahead, and it felt like he was suddenly speeding down the road. I'll never forget how white his knuckles were as he gripped the steering wheel. I think without saying anything he was reminding my mother and me that you and your father were working somewhere out there, off the very road we were driving down, working for that market. I looked down at my hands for a long time, the back of my neck and thighs drenched in sweat; I didn't even want to see the market when we passed by. When I looked up, I saw a brown field out in the distance, a potato picker rumbling dust clouds, and then a lone horse pulling a wagon, and behind the wagon a group of men bending over, tossing potatoes onto the wagon. I thought I saw you; and for a moment I had this sudden pull in my heart, feeling my father was out there too.

Ernest looked at her with a sense of knowing, his head still and straight, as if understanding, perhaps for the first time, how their lives and memories were never that far apart.

I looked up to your father. The way he worked, and even in his worst moments of drinking I saw his grace, his need to acknowledge the force of a past and a desire for a full life.

Hmmm . . . Ernest shook his head up and down, his lips closed to a pensive smile.

I'm sorry . . . I know it wasn't easy for you, Ernest; but I don't even know my father, and I would've given anything to see him come through the door from work or from drinking, even if he were dusty, tired, or stumbling drunk against the door. We all need our own heroes.

Ernest rubbed the side of her face with the back of his hand, wiping away her tears. He leaned over, kissed both of her cheeks, then her lips.

Magdalene told him: And I've come to feel that what I've struggled with is not aloneness. I know that feeling, I've felt it, and I remember your growing up. I think I'm afraid of that next little step or moment, that little leap into life: I'll simply be who I can be.

Yes, that's it, Magdalene. I try to tell myself that a lot—I'm no worse or any better than anyone else, but I am me, you are you. I wish I knew your father.

I once thought you might know. We always told each other everything, though, so I thought: Ernest would tell me if he knew.

I would; I will. I promise, if I ever find out I'll tell you. It's odd, I always wondered why my father never spoke of you or your mother very much.

Can you blame him?

No; but I guess it made me think either he was hiding a secret, or he didn't know much about your mother's life.

She shook her head in agreement. They both took another sip.

Can I ask you a question, though?

Of course, she said.

Ernest stretched his legs, leaned back on his hands, the night sky brightening his white shirt, the birch tree behind him.

Do I seem okay? Ah, I don't know what I want to ask . . . *Do I seem okay—walking down the street—I'm okay?* They both laughed in a sudden instance of recognition; Ernest had twisted his face up in an exaggerated drunk pose, a gesture from the fifth grade when he once came to a school Halloween party dressed as a hobo. Now, his face straightened, he looked into her eyes.

I mean, in our letters, meeting briefly again today, do you like who I am?

Yes—I do. You are Ernest. You've changed, you're different, like I said earlier. But listen, Ernestito, I always knew there were many things you could do, and so I still see my friend—a little bit of him, a little bit of something new, a little bit of something only you can discover.

Thank you, Magda. It's a little like the collages your students will make?

91

Nice. I like that. She leaned over, rested her head on his chest, her arm over his stomach. She listened to the waves softly tumbling into the stone-covered beach.

Ernest shivered, her head shaking on his chest. He crossed his arm over her shoulder, still shivering. She lifted up.

Are you cold?

Just a little. Maybe I should put on my coat.

No, here. Magdalene stood, moved the wineglasses from the throw, and motioned for Ernest to step off; then she lifted the throw and wrapped it around his shoulders. She held him and rubbed his back briskly.

How's that?

Better.

Come on then, she said, taking his hand, and they ran down the hill, crossed the road, still shoeless, and only stopped when their feet hit stones, pine needles. They both hopped around, walked gingerly on their tiptoes. There was a group of people sitting by a bonfire on the beach. They joined the group in front of the fire, raising their feet up toward the flames; the heat was too much, but Magdalene held her right foot up to it, turning it, letting the heat warm it slowly. Then she raised her left.

Hey, Magdalene.

She could make out Dorothy, one of the girls from her room, sitting on a log with some others, a green bottle of beer, shiny from the flames, in her hand. Magdalene waved back.

She took Ernest's hand, and they walked down the beach toward another bonfire. She paused on the edge of a dark clump of pines and birches just off the lake. She pulled Ernest close, her right leg between his feet, her thigh against his groin. She kissed him, his hands running along her ribs, her breasts, returning her kiss. They let go of each other, then she took his hand and they stepped into the trees and spread out the throw.

She heard a carriage coming down the road, the wheels turning with a *creak creak*, then the clomping of hooves, jingling bells. She undressed, Ernest watching her, his hands swaying at his sides, the moon falling through the trees in patches of white that brightened her thighs, her hands, the pattern of cattails and ducks on the throw. Goosebumps rose along her shoulders, down the back of her calves, her heart filling with the full moon. Ernest stepped forward, took her in his arms, and kissed her; first her lips, then her shoulder and collarbone, and then he took her left nipple in his mouth. Still in his clothes—his white shirt seeming painted on his body in the moonlight—he fell to his knees, his tongue running along her stomach, her thighs, and then his face all of a sudden soft and warm between her legs. She touched the top of his head, his face moving closer, his hands holding the back of her thighs.

She looked up at the moon, let Ernest discover where he needed to be, the trees shaking with the wind off the lake, the leaves little silver fishes darting through heavy currents. The stars watched them, she knew, and she wanted them to see her and Ernest in this current, surging into each other, and feeling that they did not need to be apart again.

Ernest kissed her stomach, stood up and held her, his belt buckle cold on her stomach. She unbuckled it, unbuttoning the bottom of Ernest's shirt. He pulled it over his head, letting his pants fall to the ground.

I've never done this before.

She followed Ernest down onto the throw. There were stones under her hands, pieces of driftwood behind his head. She sat on Ernest's thighs and helped him find his way within her, the smell of pine surrounding their hands, their lips, the shape of their movements and gestures, the shaking leaves above them changing—for the briefest of moments—from currents to the tender music of a lone guitar.

That's okay—it's one piece we'll glue to our lives.

Magdalene rose and fell into Ernest, their hipbones meeting briefly with each surge, each strum, a branch touching the top of her head when she rose, the moon a white stripe across Ernest's chest, his face in the shadows of the trees. She rose and fell into Ernest, hearing bells, the crack of wood splitting in a fire, their hipbones finding each other. She held Ernest's shoulders, the branch rubbing her head each time she rose, the sound of the lake guiding them together, waves returning again and again, and then hooves on the road echoing in her ears, Ernest's hand on the small of her back, Magdalene becoming a green guitar full of moon and sea and music.

They stood up and wrapped themselves in the throw. They held each other tightly, their heat surrounding them. Her legs quivered as they stepped to the edge of the trees. She heard laughter, *ooh . . . ahh*, more laughter, and then a bonfire suddenly jumped up with tall flames and she saw a girl run down the shore followed by a boy. In the distance, traveling through the blues of the night, seeming to break free from the dark steel of the Mackinac Bridge, a tanker slowly cut through the straits.

We should get dressed, no?

She felt Ernest's lips on her ear, and his hand softly playing her back.

Yes, Ernest, let's, she said.

They finished dressing, folded the throw, and gingerly walked back across the stones and pine needles. They picked up their belongings and filled her bike's basket. The wine bottle was empty.

Did you bring anything to drink? Magdalene asked.

Ernest took a silver flask from his coat pocket. The sweet sugar and bright spice and citrus of the rum warmed her mouth all the way down to the deep pocket of her stomach. She passed it back to Ernest. They kissed the kiss of oranges. She held Ernest's hand and led him down the road away from town. Bats swerved down from the higher rock caves, circling around their heads, and became black waves in the moonlight. They turned off the main road and followed a trail up West Bluff to the cottage.

Ernest dropped his bag on the floor, just as he stepped through the cottage door. He took a small sip from his flask; he handed it to her. He didn't say a word; his hands were curled, as if he were trying to hold on to the air, and his face was filled with a kind of wonder. He stepped to the desk and raised the copy of Lardner's stories, opening the cover.

You asked me to keep it for you, remember?

Yes.

In the morning I need to go down to the library for a bit, so you can use that desk if you want.

Okay. Turn off the light. Come here, Magda.

They looked out the window, down beyond the moonlit field, the sparkling waves, a lone sailboat white and clear in the night.

It's beautiful, and it will be beautiful in the morning. Ernest squeezed her, kissed the side of her head. They lay down on the bed.

Are you tired?

I'm not sure . . . Thirsty, though. Do you have any water?

She leaned over the side of the bed, opened her backpack, reached in, and handed him a bottle of water. He took a long drink. They were silent, his arms flat on the bed, her head on his chest. She listened to the crickets, heard in the distance the ringing of a boat's rigging, and fell asleep to the waves, the slow rising and falling of Ernest's chest.

The sun was high, the front of the cottage filled with light when Magdalene awoke. She found she was underneath the blanket, Ernest lying on
top in a pair of shorts, his hands tucked under his chin. He must have
gotten up in the middle of the night and undressed, she thought. She
slipped out of bed quietly. She took her backpack outside to the shower.
She showered, dressed, and then wrote a small note telling Ernest to
come down to the library, to use the shower, make himself at home, read
for a bit, and come down when he liked. She stuck the note on the door,
closing it softly.

Magdalene rode down West Bluff, her legs feeling strong each time she
pushed down with the pedals, past the Grand Hotel, the bike racks shiny
and full with silver and black, the smell of cut grass and manure drifting
in the air, and then she went through the long archway of trees shading
the road down the hill, her hair full of the air, her eyes watering. Before
she went to the library she stopped at the Yacht Club, the only place
on the island to buy decent, real clothes. They had just opened, Can-
dace flipping the OPEN sign over. Magdalene walked in and went down
through the men's aisle, letting her hands brush against the clothes folded
on the shelves. I'm looking for color, she thought. Ernest had arrived in
that black suit, a bit worn and shiny, and probably one of several he had
bought at a secondhand store. She came upon a white button-down with

long, thin, royal blue stripes. Up on the shelf above was a maroon V-neck sweater of merino wool, soft and luxurious, the weave tight, not too heavy, she thought, perfect for a cool evening. She tucked the folded shirt into the sweater, matching their colors. They went well together; not a perfect match so Ernest wouldn't look overly self-conscious about his clothes, Magdalene thought, but nice together, and he can wear them together or separately with his suit. She took them up front to pay.

Outside, on Main Street, there were small patches of white fog winding around the verandah of the Lakefront Hotel, the air of the lake this morning cool yet already filling with the day's sun. A wagon passed by as she placed the bag in the front basket of her bike, the old horse clomping hard on the road, pulling a load of groceries down to the market; Magdalene's nose filled with the scent of pine, her hands felt stones, Ernest. She touched her face, pinched the tip of her nose, and laughed inside.

She noticed the people leaving the hotels were beginning to mill out onto the streets. Workers swept the freshly sprayed sidewalks and shoveled up manure and bits of hay. She jumped on her bike and rode down to the library.

Mary had taped yellow and blue balloons to the outside columns. She had brought out a small table lined with books and copies of *National Geographic*, and, written in red on a piece of construction paper taped to the table, FREE TO TAKE. And underneath that, ANNUAL BOOK SALE: MORE PLEASURABLE READING TREASURES INSIDE. Magdalene spotted the cracked, faded *Webster's Dictionary* on the table as she passed. There were a few people browsing the inside tables. Mary sat behind the counter, a small cigar box to her side.

Did your beau make it over?

Sure did.

How'd it go?

Wonderful; and thanks for the wine.

Mary smiled, handed Magdalene a cup of coffee. She handed Mary the bag from the Yacht Club and asked her to put it behind the counter. Magdalene turned to the books, straightened out a few piles, and then took some money from a woman who bought four novels. Most of the morning they continued to take money, make change, straighten out books, watch small groups of people come and go. No one checked out a book all morning.

Around eleven Ernest walked in, his white shirt rolled to his elbows, the blue index cards Magdalene had left for him in the cottage and a pen tucked into his pocket. His face was a little red. He nodded, raised his forefinger in a wave.

You're turning red.

I can feel it, he said; it is cool out there, but the sun's still strong.

Yes, and the color's very becoming.

If I was rich, I think I'd buy one of those sailboats in the harbor. What do you think? he said, his left hand lifting up his elbow, his chin resting in the palm of his right hand.

Magdalene stepped around the corner, raised her hands to his face.

It's not your style—you're a walker, not a sailor. He kissed the back of her hand.

So this must be Ernest?

Ernest and Magdalene turned, Mary behind the counter, her right eyebrow raised in a question mark.

Mary, I'd like for you to meet Ernest. He's an old friend. Ernest extended his hand from across the counter; they shook hands.

I've heard a lot about you; the PhD is the way to go—you'll have a chance to do so much with it. Especially given what Magdalene has told me.

Ernest looked at her with astonishment; then he looked at Magdalene, his face turning into a questioning smile.

We'll have to see; but thanks for the encouragement. It would be a good feeling to do rewarding work, to be surrounded with even a fraction of these books, Ernest said, pointing and creating a half circle around the room.

How was your morning? Magdalene asked.

He pulled the index cards from his pocket, turned them to Mary and her, and spread them out like playing cards, each filled with writing.

I had a little coffee, he told them, then I sat at the desk—the view was spectacular. He lifted a card and read, *Painters teach us to see*. It is not the exact quote but I remember it from van Gogh's letters, and your window, Magda, taught me to see this morning. He straightened up the cards, slipped them back into his pocket.

You can thank Mary for the cottage.

Oh, don't thank me at all . . .

Ernest interrupted—Oh, but *thank you*.

She nodded, lowered her eyes briefly, and then smiled.

Why only for the weekend; couldn't Magdalene rent it for fall, while she's up here teaching?

Magdalene said, No, and began to add that she—but Mary said, Well, I don't see why not. Magdalene didn't mention it to me, but it will be empty all fall as far as I know. Let me ask the owners.

Magdalene, Ernest said, that's what I would do; whatever it costs, treat yourself. It will be a wonderful place for you to live this fall.

She didn't know what to say, yet she felt he was right: *I will live in the cottage this fall, I will live with my memory of Ernest's visit and his thinking of me*. She nodded yes. She asked Mary to hand her the bag from behind the counter.

For you—a treat.

Ernest looked at her strangely. Magdalene pushed the bag against his stomach, twice, and then tentatively he took it.

But why?

You'll see.

He opened the bag, looked in, closed it, smiled, and then opened it again and pulled out the shirt and sweater.

These are gorgeous.

You need more color, boy. And Ernestito, when you walk down the streets in these colors you won't have to ask, *Do I seem okay?*

He chuckled, his lips opening, his teeth bright, then tucking them under his lips as he laughed. Ernest pointed to the men's room across the room. He lifted his hand to her face, held her cheek, and mouthed a *thank you*.

After he entered the men's room Mary said, He seems very nice, Magdalene. I think you do have a beau.

She shook her head. *I think so*.

Suddenly the library was full, a large group of college students hurrying through the twentieth-century novels, a couple perusing the history section, and more people entering, the front door continuing to click open. The sun was higher, the great room of the library filled with warm light. A young boy walked up to the counter with a stack of *National Geographic*s in his arms and asked Mary if it was okay for him to take them. She told him, Sure, as many as you like.

When Ernest came out of the men's room there was a line of people with books waiting to pay. Magdalene took a five from a young woman, gave her back her change. She looked up, and Ernest stood there with a hand in his pocket, the other lightly pulling up his shirt collar, then smoothing down the front of his sweater. *What do you think?* he mouthed from across the room. She took some money from an elderly woman, giving Ernest an okay sign. The old woman looked behind her, then back at Magdalene, wondering what was going on.

Thank you, Magdalene said, and have a great day.

When she looked up again, Ernest was browsing through the books, and then she saw his hand jump, a *Wow!* appearing on his face. He lifted up the book, opened it. *Wow!* again. The line started to dwindle, and then Ernest was next in line.

How much for this book, miss? he asked. Before she could answer Mary stepped over to the counter.

Today, for you, that's free.

Are you sure? Look at this—Ernest held the book in front of them, the cover open—it is a nice edition of *Jane Eyre*.

Sure, go ahead.

Thank you. Ernest handed Magdalene the bag with his white shirt. He pointed outside to the back porch, and she waved for him to go ahead.

Magdalene helped Mary for another half hour or so, business beginning to slow down after noon. She went and straightened the piles of books again. Mary told her to leave them, that she should get going before the afternoon slipped away. Magdalene stepped over to the back door but stopped for a moment. Ernest sat in a white rocking chair, his book open on his lap, a blue index card filled with notes in the palm of his hand, his pen between his fingers, poised just above the card. He squinted, looked out on the freshwater sea, lost in a thought, maybe some memory. The royal blue stripes added great color to his darkening face, and the sweater was even more luxurious than she had thought, the way the white and blue of his shirtsleeves hit his wrist, just below the small folded sleeves of his sweater.

That was what Magdalene remembered the most. His colors. His quiet contemplation. A feeling of happiness she had always been searching for, running toward: *Seeing him, feeling him close, the sensation that nothing will deny that he's Ernest, that I'm Magdalene, that we are who we are because of the shame and fear, the hate and bitterness, the awful glue of loneliness and pain that was such a powerful force in our lives. And that we are even more because of it.*

Ernest raised his pen in the air, and perhaps not caring if anyone saw him, he pointed it toward the sea, striking invisible points or notes, all the while his lips moving, and then his hand began to slowly shape a pattern, back and forth, and Magdalene thought she heard his pen touching the music of the waves roaring into the stony shore.

Ernest rented a bike and they rode around the island. They sat in the park below the fort and watched the people play Frisbee and sunbathe. They ate slices of pizza and drank a few beers. They rode down to Mission Point and sat late into the afternoon in the white Adirondack chairs the Mission had spread across the lawn, looking out onto the lake, talking, holding hands, and taking turns reading pages from *Jane Eyre*. When evening arose, Ernest took Magdalene's hand and walked her over to the clubhouse just off the lake, and they sat at a bistro table under a heat lamp and ate dinner—wine, salad, hot bread, thick slices of butter, steak, and, amazingly, they had soft shell crabs. They ate with great relish. Once again their mouths crunched with batter and shell as the sun was setting behind them. They decided to ride around the island once again, their guides on the dark road the bats, the light of the stars, and the full moon a bright lamp on the surface of the lake, each wave shimmering with silver. They were exhausted in the cottage, and both sunburned. They held each other with tenderness, the cotton sheets painful against their skin as they gently made love.

That was what she remembered most. *His hand on the small of my back. Those colors. My head resting perfectly on his high chest. The Miles Davis tune we played over and over again. His quiet contemplation.*

But then there was more: Ernest standing by the window in the middle of the night, naked, his body white with the moonlight, and the cottage's wooden floor like a clear and cool pool of water. She rose up on her arm.

Ernest?

Yes? He still looked out the window, down toward the sea.

What are you doing?

He turned away from the window, his head turning toward the floor. In profile she could see his erection, and he tried to push himself down with his hand. Magdalene's heart leaped for him; she felt the need to help him raise his head high. He hugged himself and then turned back to the window.

I was thinking of you and me on the beach, he said, and I couldn't sleep . . . my stomach was on fire, and . . . I don't know, it's just these days have gone by too fast and . . . he stopped. He turned his head back down toward the floor again, as if he felt embarrassed or dejected.

Magdalene slipped out of bed quietly, stepping into the moonlight. She wrapped her arms around him and said: The lake is here in the room with us—all that water. She listened to waves crashing into the stony shore.

Yes—a freshwater sea rising into our room.

Magdalene repeated those words, *our room*.

Our room, Ernest, yes it is our best room, she told him; and maybe we can keep it with us forever. She rubbed his stomach, and held him; her thighs pressing against his. She let go of him, took a few steps backward, and lay down on the floor in the moonlight.

She called him from the floor.

He turned around and looked at her; she could not see his eyes but felt them on her legs, her stomach.

Ernest, come with me before the moon and sea leave our room.

The next day at noon, Ernest stood on the back of the ferry, his shirt and sweater bright with color in the sun. He looked down on the water, squinting, and then his contemplation was broken. He raised his hand, palm open. Magdalene waved good-bye, an arc of golden light becoming a rainbow over the back of the ferry as it turned from the harbor, Ernest's color lost. She saw him running for a moment, trying to stay within her line of sight, but she was left with only a brief glimpse of his hand, glinting, enveloped by gold, blue, and then disappearing.

The mountains had been golden earlier this evening, the grasses and trees taking in the day's sun, the cattle grazing on the plateau looking like deep red mounds glinting in the fields. A motorcycle somewhere in the distance hit a curve, slowed down, then picked up speed, its motor whining high. It was cool tonight, a small strip of fog drifting in off the shore, a half moon curved around the bottom edge of the darkening valley. Abuela had placed a small radio in the window, and Magdalene watched as the tubes warmed to an orange glow, the music coming out clear, fantastic, and full of feeling: now a lone guitar strummed galloping horses into the evening. On the table beside them were the two short glasses of cane whiskey Abuela had filled. She finished rolling two cigarettes and handed one to Magdalene.

The men in our family could never handle their drinking. Abuela lifted the bottle.

A bottle like this they'd want to drink racing, in a couple of mouthfuls.

She placed the bottle down on the table. Handed Magdalene a glass.

Salud.

They took small sips from their glasses; the whiskey burned Magdalene's tongue, then became sweet and warm as it glided down her throat.

Tastes good, ha? Abuela asked.

Magdalene nodded, licked her lips.

I've had this bottle it seems forever; I take it slow. A couple of nights a week, for almost twenty-five years now, I sit down, listen to a little music, sip slowly and pleasantly with a cigarette. It clears the mind, lets me know what I want from life, the very next day.

She struck a match against a box, inhaled. She slowly guided the match in front of Magdalene's face. When Magdalene exhaled she focused on a lone avocado tree bathed in shadow, a gold circle of sunlight caught in its leaves, and, circling back and forth from shadow and light, yellow butterflies.

Maybe that's helping you to live a strong life, Magdalene said.

Maybe . . . It is hard to say how long anyone will have a chance to see butterflies like that, Abuela said, pointing her cigarette at the avocado tree; and in a beautiful, inspiring moment of change, the sun shifted and the tree was completely enveloped by shadow and the butterflies instantly disappeared.

Abuela said, We are here, and this is very fine, one of the first times you and I have been alone.

Yes, very fine.

You remind me a lot of your mother, you know.

You *knew* my mother? Magdalene asked.

Ramóna Crespo, sure I did. I was just remembering how your mother sat in that same chair drinking mango juice, and how her mother sat there as well, talking to me just like you are.

Really?

Yes, many times. Your mother lived down the road, up on the side of the mountain, down that little side road that curves into the valley—and I knew her mother, your abuela, Magdalene Crespo, well. And how could I not? I felt responsible to help her in any way I could.

What do you mean?

Your abuela gave birth to your mother out of wedlock; and though she knew who the father was, she wouldn't tell. Your mother was so light skinned, lily-white as they say, that a rumor began: people gossiped and said her father was one of the American soldiers from Arecibo who always liked to come to the beaches in Rincon. Though I'm not sure how many actually believed this gossip.

Abuela took a deep drag, exhaled through her nose.

What happened is that the community pushed your abuela aside; they decided she could stand for all the young women who gave birth to children without husbands, even though they turned a blind eye to what was happening; most of the men had left for the mainland to find work. Remember, back then everybody was very poor. I did what I could; I shared extra food, gave her some old baby clothes, and I talked to your abuela when no one else would.

Abuela scratched the back of her hand, took another drag of her cigarette, the tobacco and paper crackling loud and orange.

And I knew your mother well because she and Ernest's father were such good friends. They were almost inseparable; playing outside in the red patch of dirt next to the ox, swimming in the stream on the edge of the cane field, climbing up the mountain for a whole day. They were schoolmates for a time.

My mother and Changó were *good friends?* Magdalene asked in total disbelief, taking a deep swallow of whiskey. Then why did she hate him so much in the states?

I'm not sure. There may have been a few things that happened. Your abuela became a little uneasy about all the time they were spending together, and I believe she may have shared some of her own bitterness with your mother. Then my husband, Ernest's abuelo, sent Changó to work in the fields. And this seemed to create changes we would all live with; it was clear, Changó would work until he was old enough to go out on his own, and then, even though this is not what his father meant to happen, Changó would leave for the mainland like so many others.

Abuela shrugged a *What can you say?*

Once your mother grew older, she decided to leave as soon as she could; I remember she and your abuela were fighting one day, I don't know about what, but I can still hear your mother yelling, *I'll be leaving and you won't have to worry about me. I'll be leaving like everyone else and you'll be all alone.* Your mother grew to hate Puerto Rico, and men like Changó, who seemed to leave so freely—

Magdalene interrupted her. But wait a minute. My father is Puerto Rican. Why did she come all the way to the mainland to repeat the same life her mother had lived?

I don't know . . . some things happen. Have you ever asked her?

Magdalene did not answer, her mind following the bats swerving in the now darkening sky, the memory of her mother's hate extinguishing any shape or pattern to what she might begin to understand.

Passion must be passion, Magdalene thought, and then she saw Ernest, naked, standing in a band of moonlight in front of a window, and she remembered how blood rushed to her chest, how her thighs seemed to shiver, and how she quietly slipped out of bed and wrapped her arms around his waist, her breasts pressing into his back.

Do you know anything of your abuela, Magdalene?

No . . . My mother never mentioned her. Not even that I was named for her.

Oh, I didn't know. Magdalene was a fine, fine woman—I could talk to her about anything. We would shop in Rincon and attend mass, too. You know, your mother left and didn't have any hard feelings toward her mother. In fact, she was planning on bringing her to the mainland, and your abuela even spoke of you before you were born. She knew your mother was pregnant and wanted to be there to help out when you were born; she told me, *I can't wait to hold her in my arms.* She believed with all her heart you would be a girl.

Abuela patted Magdalene's hand.

That year we had terrible heavy rains and mudslides. Muy peligroso. I begged your abuela to come down off the mountain and stay with us for a bit. She didn't want to trouble us. Her house went down in a mudslide one evening. They searched and searched but never found her.

Night had arisen; a silver glow from the phosphorescent bay sparkled and waved on the horizon.

Look out there, Abuela said. She's still there somewhere.

Magdalene looked into the night and listened to the coquis; she thought of how their sounds had become so familiar, and how each night she gave them a little more of her fear, and then she listened as the coquis released it forever into the night through their song. There was not a name, she thought, for that place, but it was out there collecting her fear. She squeezed the deep pocket of her stomach, released, listened. She squeezed Abuela's forearm, let her hand linger on her flesh, this living connection to her mother, her abuela. There's many different parts I'll never glue together, she thought, and then she drifted in memory: *Where did that metaphor come from, what are these pieces, this glue?*

Ernest had said to her, *It's a little like the collages your students will make?*

He was underneath her, his hips smooth and warm, his hand on the small of her back. She told him, *That's okay—it's one piece we'll glue to our lives.*

Abuela pointed to Magdalene's glass.

Here, let me give you a little more. Abuela filled her glass halfway, and Magdalene passed by a sip, taking a nice long drink.

You mind if I ask you a question, Magdalene?

No, go right ahead.

She turned her head, stared at Magdalene, who felt like she was asking, *Are you sure?*

Go ahead, anything—like drinking this whiskey, we take it straight, no chaser.

Abuela nodded, a *hmmm* rising from her mouth.

I wonder. You're a smart woman, you could have much in your life. Ernest is my grandson; Isabel my first great-granddaughter. I wonder why you and Ernest are not together?

Magdalene took another drink. She rested the glass on her thigh, then lifted it and swirled the whiskey around, the small light from the radio in the window a mellow gold in the whiskey, shaking to the sound of the cymbals she now heard.

He doesn't know Isabel is his daughter; I never told him.

And can I ask why not?

Abuela's voice was a little hoarse, Magdalene thought, maybe even a little astonished or angry. She searched for an answer, tried to find the truth in her mind.

I was—I am still, often—afraid. He was becoming someone he liked, for once, and I was afraid he'd hate me for changing his life.

Shouldn't you let him decide? Abuela asked.

Often I thought the same thing. You have to understand—I dreamed he could be happy and love Isabel . . . maybe love me. I would then be filled with doubt. What if he decided one day just to leave. How could I live with that pain?

You could, mija; what else could you do? Abuela began rolling another cigarette, a little thicker and fatter than her last one, taking her time with the paper. She licked the edge, smoothing the paper with the tips of her fingers.

I hear what you mean: there's too much memory, too much blood, telling us how bitter and hateful our lives can be, Abuela said. She struck a match, inhaled, and passed the cigarette to Magdalene. Abuela held her chin, slowly exhaling.

You've been here maybe five months or so, and the whole time you've been welcomed. I love having the both of you here; and you can stay as long as you like. When Changó came here with Ernest, they stayed almost a year, and the whole time I told him he couldn't run away from his pain, he had to find a way to live with it and without it. ¿Tu me entende?

Yes, I do. Absolutely. Magdalene took another drag of the cigarette, handing it back to Abuela.

I also told him that even though he might sometimes feel lonely, even though he might want to live here in Puerto Rico again, he had started a life with someone else he needed to return to—and, even if he was afraid they may not stay together, he couldn't know unless he tried. First he had to take Ernest home, quit drinking, and then he might begin to know the life he and Evelyn could live together. As I think you know, he did the first thing, took Ernest home, and then it took many, many years for him to quit drinking and begin the rest of his life.

Abuela reached across the small space between them, touched the side of Magdalene's face, and then motioned with her hand, *Drink up.*

Magdalene tipped the glass to her lips, finished her whiskey.

There were many times I wanted to call Ernest and tell him. Many times I called because I needed his help. And then I'd think too much time had passed . . . Isabel is too old . . . he'd say now it's too late. But right now, if some woman spoke in the darkness, and you said that's the voice of my abuela, I'd run out into the field with my arms wide open. We'd hold each other just in time.

A slow, almost quiet piano came over the radio. The composition Latin, and yet after a few more bars Magdalene recognized the song as "Somewhere Over the Rainbow."

Abuela raised her hands off her lap, let her fingers dance to the song. She smiled, tapped Magdalene's thigh. She pointed into the night.

She's out there. She'll always wait to hold you. And I can't say, but maybe Ernest is waiting for someone to hold him. We'll never know unless someone tries, right?

That's right, Magdalene said to herself, *unless I try*.

And remember what you said about time, mija. It's not too late; we can sit here and clear our minds, let each other know what we want from life, decide the very next thing we want to do tomorrow.

He wrote to me. I wrote to him. We talked of what we most enjoyed about seeing each other. He had a break in November and told me he'd like to visit again. His letters were beautiful; his words contained a lyrical excitement I couldn't get enough of. He wrote of how he came back from the island filled with energy, was working hard every day, and how intense and vivid his afternoon walks were. I had to slowly live in his letters; they placed me in particularly stunning landscapes, caught perfectly an idea or feeling found in certain light-filled objects, human gestures, the patina of gutters and roofs, and the sound of wind rushing down an alley, through steel bridges. I wrote back in August, in September, but in late October I woke up in the mornings sick to my stomach and throwing up. Then I recalled what my mother had said to me when I was entering the eleventh grade: If you don't stay away from him you'll end up in bad shape, throwing up—a disgrace. You'll get pregnant, Magda, and he'll leave you. They all leave.

He continued to write, would ask why I didn't write back, and then he wrote that I must be busy with my teaching and asked how it was going, asked again how the collages had turned out. He wrote a letter I couldn't bear to keep. The weather had turned colder, wet, and often horrible for walking. He walked as much as he could, he said, but he now spent a lot of time reading, especially van Gogh's letters again, and he liked to go to *the Art Institute as much as possible. In the letter he included a powerful description of a young boy on a sorrel horse:*

The fall to the soil of a plump mango from a heavy afternoon rain, the birth of a clear azure sky broken by torn, puffy clouds, the sky sparkling on the baked red-clay-dirt road; and then coming toward me is a young boy with no shirt, his skin is a little darker than the dirt, his jeans streaked with dust all the way down to his bare feet, and when he pulls back on a hemp rope bridle he and a sorrel horse gently trot by, the boy's black hair slick and still, the horse's neck taut, severe, without regret, its blond mane barely fluttering in the breeze stirring off the sea.

He said it was a memory he had shared with Lorime before he died— but I felt it was for me. I had to hold it close.

The letter was filled with such a light quickness, a kind of running, where Ernest was facing his life, catching important things that were guiding him in profound ways, helping him to become.

There was this moment when he tried to explain how he felt, why he wished I would write to him. He told me, Something more than our past, more than your beauty and friendship, Magdalene, arose in Mackinac. I am in love with you, and I can say it.

I don't remember it all; I no longer have the letter; I couldn't hold on to it any longer, my hands on fire with his words. I walked out of the cottage, the letter pressed against my stomach, and then I held the letter between my hands and ripped it into little pieces, let the wind carry it down below, through the birch trees, over the pines, and into the freshwater sea.

I never answered his letters.

I called him.

I listened to his voice but I could not speak.

Even when he called my name, Magda, Magdalene, is that you again? Please, Magdalene, talk to me? Let me know what . . .

I held my stomach, Isabel's kicks harder inside me. I put the phone down.

I had by then moved back to my parents', spent as much time as possible alone in my bedroom, the door closed. Outside my window, in the evening light, I heard my mother's chair creak in her garden, her deep, sorrowful sigh, and then the old fallen leaves of fall rising crisply in the wind. The scent of the blooming dogwoods. The tumbling river. All the robins happy with spring. Then a voice coming from I don't know where as I called out to her, Who's my father, huh?

She'd lift from her chair, scream, Comemierda, eat shit, he can comemierda. I told you what would happen . . . I told you . . . her voice circling over and over again, wild with hate, her anger quieting the leaves until she finally gave up in exhaustion.

Who's my grandmother, huh? Why can't you tell me who she is? Who's my grandfather? What are you afraid of? Why can't you even tell me their names? I'd grab my stomach, lift my legs off the ground, the pain deep but almost gratifying as I began to cry.

My mother would yell back, In the dirt, she's in the dirt . . . They're all dirty, filthy, muddy . . .

Ernest finished that last year of his master's, pushed himself for three years and earned his PhD. Isabel turned four years old just about the same time he graduated. I told Juan I was going to visit my mother but drove instead to the South Shore train station. In the bathroom I dressed Isabel in a nice dark blue dress, yellow ribbons in her hair, and I stepped into a sleeveless dress of a similar shade, a yellow scarf around my neck, a white sweater on my shoulders. We took the train to Chicago. I hoped just to see him, for Isabel and I to offer our congratulations. Out of all those family members and friends in the crowd he wouldn't know, I wanted to be the only person from his past; and for Isabel to be a new, happy presence in his life. I panicked when we arrived. He had taken a job, would soon leave Chicago and begin to take that next little leap into his life, and all I could do was stand out of his way. I took Isabel down to Navy Pier, and we got some lunch. We looked out onto the lake, eating ice cream. I pushed her on a swing and she was happy. We were in Chicago for maybe two hours and then took the train back, Isabel asleep on my lap, her breath warm and steady, all I needed so I wouldn't cry. Outside, the countryside turned gold and then blue as the sun moved west.

I yelled, inside some nameless countryside of my mind, No te pures, don't you worry, Mamí, I let Ernest go. I'm nothing like you—I let him go, he didn't leave me like my father left you.

Part Three

Ernest

The birch trees swayed in the breeze, their silver undersides stirring, the grass below a deep green brightened by yellow tulips. A robin hopped from branch to branch, my ears and fingertips beginning to sting from the breeze. I shifted my bag from one hand to another, stumbled for a moment under the trees, my stomach in my throat, my nose burning with the leftover taste of rum. I closed my eyes, made a fist and punched myself in the stomach, just under my ribs, and then the pain caused me to open my eyes, focus; I stood and let the silver undersides of trees stay with me a little longer and hoped they'd shape the ways I saw this evening.

It was close to five thirty, and Abuela Lacasa's plane should have landed. I walked to my car thinking, *One more week to finish this first year . . . one more week and maybe, and just maybe this year—with all its change and death—will be over.* Then I found myself drifting off further: Boogaloo's ashes. My father sitting in a brightly colored garden, his eyes covered by patches. Isabel and Magdalene walking alone along a sandy beach, collecting bright shells of white and pink. How I wanted them to be here with me. I needed to make Magdalene understand: *We were in love, and we still can create more love, though we won't know what our love is unless you let me try, Magda.*

Starting my car, I released the front latches for the top and then lowered it. The sun flooded the inside, my legs warm, a wave of cool air on my face, my neck. *Forget about last night*, I told myself; *just don't let that happen again*. I lifted Boogaloo from the passenger-side floorboard and placed him in a patch of sunlight on the seat. On long Fridays like today, I often found myself wondering how long they would allow me to teach here, how long would they pay me for this great luxury, this dream some call work. In those moments I'd become filled with a sad dread, return to my memory of the fields, and then my loneliness would well up inside, my throat chock-full of heart. I wouldn't leave my office—I'd stay because of my fear, afraid that once I got outside the only thing to calm my heart would be drink. Turning on a lamp, sitting in the Friday-evening light that turned my office half blue, half orange, I'd go without dinner and work late into the night on papers, read a book, watch the sun disappear outside my window, as I wrote another letter to Magdalene. A single, older colleague would often come by, knock lightly on the door, and we'd talk about how things were going. *Okay. Great. It has its good and its bad.* He'd tell me not to worry. Just try to enjoy the time.

I did that. Yet I would never call it joy; my life and work needed to reach for much more to survive. *Don't feel this way—don't feel shame. Good work is good work*, Boogaloo had once told me. I listened to him again.

Boogaloo stopped, his hand raised to his mouth.

How you say it, ante de memoria? You know, after memory?

Yes, after. But you might also mean before. No?

Segudo. You know what I mean. We have to live ante de memoria . . .

I wrapped my orange and red scarf around my neck. I felt the pull of a new field of memory: *I'll walk through the tall grass with some books in my hand, some blue index cards and a pen in my shirt pocket, and even though I won't be exerting physical labor, men like Boogaloo and my father will shape the exact arc of my gestures. I'll walk through the tall grass of the field with my memories, with Magdalene and Isabel close by, with the rest of the day ahead of us.*

Pulling out of the parking lot, I shifted into second, picked up speed, shifted into third, the mixture of sun and wind suddenly refreshing, exhilarating, and my hangover not so harsh. With forty-five minutes to go before Abuela Lacasa's arrival party, I decided to drive out to the Johansen property.

The road along the bay was empty, the water cobalt blue, a line of short white waves curving at the shoreline. I shifted into fifth gear, the speedometer at fifty-five, only ten miles over the speed limit, the birch trees whipping by, the air fresh on my face and filled with pine, wet stones, water. I heard a seagull and then watched old leaves drifting in front of the car and striking the top of the windshield with a bright, high crack. Braking, I downshifted and hit the sharp curve on my way out across the peninsula. About a half a mile in I turned to the left, downshifted to second, the road curving and twisting through a thick, tall pine forest, the road flat with black shadows, small circles and squares of sunlight breaking up the shadows, the darkness of tree trunks, a rhythm emerging from these dark and light patterns as I gently turned the wheel, my hips following each tight curve. I reached the top of the road, looked out on the high hills of the peninsula, an amber gold in the late afternoon light. I accelerated; shifted into neutral, glided down the road. About a quarter of a mile from the Johansen property, I tapped the brakes lightly and pulled in next to a row of poplar trees, their newly arrived leaves shaking above me.

I got out of the car, slowly and quietly, and closed the door. I stepped to the side of a tree and looked out across the field. There was a small, two-story Victorian cottage, white with beige trim around the eaves, the shingles gold, glinting in the sun. All the windows covered with plywood. The second floor had a front room with two windows; I looked at those windows, saw the tables I could place against each window, a window for Magdalene and one for me, both of us looking down on this field. A room for Isabel, too. The main floor had a picture window and a split-rail porch made of thin ornate timbers. All the windows were trimmed in Victorian woodwork, tiny little roofs above each window, as if each window was an individual replica of the cottage's facade.

I listened to the lake caught in the wind, the leaves, and then heard the tall grasses swaying in the lake's wind. It was the first time I noticed how the cottage was bathed in light at this moment in the day; the front of the cottage, facing southeast, covered with amber-mottled shadows, and the left side, facing northwest, full of sunlight. One Sunday in March, I was out on an afternoon drive and discovered this cottage. I've been driving here ever since, watching the snow melt away, green grass appearing, trees beginning to bud, the birds becoming louder and more abundant as they swerved across my line of vision, the birch and alder and pine woods behind the cottage becoming fuller, more defined in their greens and whites and blacks.

I often wondered why the cottage was all alone, why no one lived here; and again I found myself standing in stunning light, dreaming I lived here, dreaming Magdalene and Isabel were looking at the tall, straight birch trees out front, planted at perfect intervals about seventy-five feet from the front porch.

My stomach was awash in nerves, my legs quivering. When the leaves above me stirred I remembered the time when Magdalene came around a birch tree outside my cabin and found me on my knees, trying to wash my dirty face after I had just thrown up. When I turned it was as if she had stepped out of the twilight, her dark hair tinted by the setting sun, her face clean and bright; and though I didn't use the word then, at the age of fifteen she was beautiful, beautiful in the way I desired now: a woman I wanted as a friend to share my days with; a woman I could sit with at a café and watch as her lips and nose moved while she spoke, her eyes filling with light and language and longing for better dreams; a woman I could sleep with every night and know that the way her chest fit on my chest was meant to be, the way waves shape a moon-curved bay of sand in the starlight. Her mother always tried to dress her in an almost too obvious and strange preppy way—but when she stood there in her tartan skirt, her bright white blouse and navy blue cardigan, a yellow ribbon in her hair, she was special and beyond compare. And I had to ruin it by letting her see me dirty and still reeking of drink.

A cloud of dust rose, then a swarming circle of cut grass—Mr. Johansen cutting the last quarter of the field. I stepped back from the tree and turned to my car, my mouth cotton dry and my stomach filled with sharp nausea. I bent at the waist and coughed, coughed again, and I tried to clear my throat when the dry heaves began again. I heaved and heaved, the water I had drunk that morning finally coming up in a few long streams, followed by yellow bile. I wiped my mouth with the back of my hand, looking down on the ground, and then tried to kick some of the old fall leaves over my mess. I stepped away and slipped into my car. Pulling away from the trees, I made a U-turn and sped away toward town.

When I pulled into La Habana the parking lot was full. Pulling back out onto the street, I found plenty of spaces, parked, raised the roof, and latched the top closed. Gonzalo Lacasa's car was in the parking lot; he must have already arrived with his mother, the long wait finally over. I placed Boogaloo back on the floorboard, pushing the box back against the seat. The family had worked all year to get Abuela Lacasa here from Cuba; went through countless agencies, meetings, and forms, many letters to Washington and Havana; and then finally she was here. Tonight they were celebrating her arrival, and it felt good to take part in it. I closed the door and locked the car. I straightened the collar on my shirt, buttoned my coat, and wiped my forehead with a handkerchief. I headed toward the front door.

Mr. Vargas immediately shouted ¡Hola! a white towel draped over his shoulder, a platter of pasteles in his hand when I stepped inside. He handed me the platter, pointed quickly to a table of five on the far left. I began to cross the space that separated me from them.

Every Monday morning I arrived at La Habana for coffee at the front table by the window, and I'd arrive once or twice a week in the evening, for dinner, La Habana becoming a refuge always filled with Mr. Vargas's warmth and joy. Mr. Vargas had moved here long ago when there were no Hispanics except for a few hundred or so migrants who came in the summer to work in the fields and orchards. He told me one day that in Havana he ran a market, and so a market it would be here, in this little building next to the freshwater sea. He could tell right away that Latin-Caribbean foodstuffs would never sell enough to make him a living in this town, so he began with a simple market—milk, cheese, eggs, canned goods, a few vegetables and fruits, and fresh-baked bread. That first summer of business, Mr. Vargas noticed all the tourists, along with those from Chicago and Detroit who owned homes in the area. He decided to specialize in Italian foods; he put in a deli, too, and made sandwiches to order. *Chico*, he had said, *business never let up. Pasta, pasta, pasta. Every day with the olive oil, the roasted red peppers, the pork sausage, the big cans of plum tomatoes*. He always had a small Hispanic aisle, but once the local Mexican population began to take hold and more migrants arrived to work, he started selling an array of foodstuffs: sazon, chorizo, dried chilies, yuca and cassava, five kinds of dried beans, avocados, mangoes, those pink and yellow soaps from his childhood that came from Bogotá and Port of Spain. He even hired a Mexican woman to make fresh tortillas; roasted adobo chicken; tamales and burritos; menudo; and my favorite, which takes its name from the name of the store, La Habana: slow-roasted pork, ham, Swiss cheese, olive oil and garlic, pickles and mustard, all placed between two pieces of French bread and grilled.

Renaldo, sitting next to Mrs. Lacasa, waved a fork in the air, a plate of rice and black beans in front of him. I waved back with my free hand, raised the platter of pasteles in the other, and gave him a grimace like *I have to fill this order*, still thinking about the place Mr. Vargas had created for himself and how I longed for my own sense of home to take shape—here, around these people, the smell of garlic and pepper and cilantro wafting through the air, the noise of silverware against dishes, and the conversation and laughter, the feeling of my feet solid and straight on the floor. Here, in this place, alongside Isabel and Magdalene.

Renaldo and Mrs. Lacasa smiled. I stepped forward and reached the table on the far left and placed the platter in the middle, removing an invisible hat from my head, bending a little at the waist, my hat in my hand upturned and held just on the edge of the table.

Thank you, they said in unison.

I felt a hand on my back.

Ay, Ernestito, you made it.

When I turned, Gonzalo handed me a short glass of rum and we shook hands.

Salud, I said, and we clinked glasses. The smell of the rum was strong, and my stomach rolled, filled with the sharp scent of the alcohol and my earlier dry heaves. I raised the glass more slowly, searching for the sugar, the lemon, the buttery pineapple, the glass against my lips. I waited for the rum's lemon to wake up my tongue, and then the sugar came through, and the hotness of it all as it slowly and smoothly made its way deep into the pocket of my stomach. *Mmmm,* I almost moaned, and my arms shook a little but my feet felt heavier and steadier on the floor, and I knew I'd be okay; I tasted how clear and clean the rum was, and my stomach continued to warm and my eyes became clearer, brighter.

Gonzalo took my arm and led me over to the table. He asked, Did you have a hard time finding the place?

We sat down.

No, not at all.

You know of this place? he asked, his eyes wide, the right side of his mustache turned up with his expression, his cheekbones high and turning a reddish brown, perhaps from the rum, perhaps from the warming spring sun. In his dark brown eyes I could see the wonder and the depth of his attention and concern for the exactness of the moment, a quality that was present each time he spoke with me. I smiled, felt a small wash of shame fill my stomach; I wanted his eyes, his attention; I no longer wanted to turn away with apprehension and shyness when I spoke to others, especially Gonzalo. Perhaps to some this wasn't much to begin to stake my life on, but it was a beginning I needed and admired: to get up every morning, to work a full day without regret, and to provide for others comforts they never had to ask for.

Mrs. Lacasa set a plate of chicken and rice in front of me; I waved my hand in front of the rising steam, let the olive oil and garlic waft into my nose, the salt and black pepper, the saffron-stained chicken, the lemon.

Thank you, Julieta.

She patted my shoulder.

Sure, I said, staring into Gonzalo's eyes; I come here all the time. Pero, Gonzalo, you always talk of forgetting Cuba, moving farther and farther away, so I never mentioned this place to you.

Of course, I see. Gonzalo raised his hands in a way that said, *No harm done.* Julieta handed Gonzalo his plate. He and I began to eat, and between bites he told me:

I believed that's what I wanted, and I thought forgetting was that easy.

Workers at the cannery asked me many days to lunch here. I always declined.

Mr. Vargas came over to our table, a glistening piece of pork on a silver tray. He placed it on the table to *oohs* and *aahs*. The white tablecloth seemed tiled with colorful, distinctly individual pieces—a charred pan filled with a mound of white rice, a deep yellow bowl of black beans, the golden chicken surrounded by browned garlic cloves and thick slices of lemon and split red onions, the platter of pork with its glistening, crispy skin speckled with coarse bits of black pepper—beginning to spill into each other.

I thought I could avoid my reasons—my hate—for leaving Cuba, Gonzalo said. Move as far away as possible. But my mother was still there; I smelled and tasted the place on my skin, no matter how many times I showered. I realized, talking to you, seeing how Renaldo is growing up so quickly—well, I understood it was not fair to deny him that past. His past, no?

I shook my head, shrugged, didn't want to answer but let him tell me.

There are many places I know he never saw; I will have to tell him about them. And hell, what was I thinking? Gonzalo picked up a chicken leg and bit into it. I had to eat.

We both laughed, wiped our greasy lips. Gonzalo filled our glasses three-quarters full with rum. We raised them and drank, this time my stomach beginning to fill with rice and beans, my mouth alive with cilantro and pepper, my nausea pushed aside, the rum welcome, my stomach dancing with lemons and pineapples, an almond tree, and then the sea.

An older woman approached wearing a long green dress with yellow mango paisleys scattered about. Her silver hair pulled back tight off her smooth forehead, and on her open hand there rested a plate. *Abuela Lacasa*. With her silver hair she must have been close to eighty, I thought; and yet her skin, the color of a new penny, was smooth as butter, like butter beginning to melt on a warm summer day, her skin ageless; it was her hands, dry and cracked, and her fingers, wrinkled and twisted, that showed her years. She opened her free hand on Gonzalo's shoulder, and he took her wrist, looking up into her face. She bent down and kissed him on the forehead. Then the lips.

For you, Ernestito. Abuela reached across the table and handed me the plate filled with roast pork, and on the side, a piece of crispy skin. My favorite.

Thank you. It's good to meet you, Señora Lacasa.

For me as well. I have heard a lot about you. Thank you for getting to know my family.

Ah, it was more them letting me become a part of their lives—like I'm a distant cousin. I picked up my glass, tapped the side with my knife. Everyone turned and then raised their glasses when I raised mine.

Wait, Wait, I said, and yelled over to Mr. Vargas, who was setting a plate on a table. He turned and looked at us, and then made his way to our table, rubbing his hands together. I poured him a short glass of rum, stood, handed it to him. I raised my glass again.

For safe arrivals, the reunion of families, and for tomorrow, the beginning of more moments like this very evening: family, friends, food, and the drink of choice, love.

Here, here rose from the crowd of diners, and then, *Salud, salud, cheers, cheers*. Glasses clinked together, and then there was a small moment of silence followed abruptly by the return of talking, bursts of laughter, happy raised voices.

So, Ernest, Gonzalo asked, did you work everything out with Mr. Johansen?

We meet in a few days—and the Johansens are coming to dinner tonight, too. We'll see how it goes.

Gonzalo shook his head.

And soon Magdalene and Isabel are coming? Julieta asked.

I think . . . I hope. Need to take care of this one last thing, and then I hope they'll come.

They will, Ernest, I can feel they will, she said.

Yes, I told myself, *they must . . . they have to; I need them*. And then the voice inside me became stronger: *My mother and father were walking out of a movie theatre, quiet within themselves, with their newfound love. I remember us, Magdalene, on a hill, sitting under some birches in the twilight, your head on my chest. What will Isabel think of me? Ernest. Ernestito. Papa. What will she call me?*

I leaned my face into my palm, held the pork skin in my other hand, my eyes filling with tears, my lips trembling against my palm. A lone tear slowly rolled from my eye, and then I felt nauseous again, as if my insides were sobbing the tears of a turbulent sea. I set the piece of pork down, took my glass, and put it to my lips.

Yesterday the sky was bright blue, the southwest wind blowing in hot and strong, a beautiful, almost summer day, and I had this strange moment of sad wonder because I hadn't heard from Magdalene, and, as often happened in the past, I felt so alone, anxious, as if there was a sheet of tin inside me, like a tin roof trembling in a strong wind, that struck my insides simply because I felt bored, without purpose. By two in the afternoon I had drunk five beers, very cold, with a slice of lime pushed down into their necks. The open book resting against my thigh had not been read in some time, and I watched the sea churn white with the wind. I listened to the waves, and when the wind stopped for a moment I heard children yelling and looked for their voices. There were two young Mexican boys in cut-off jeans, without shoes or shirts, one with his red T-shirt tucked into his back pocket. They stood close to the water, trying to skip stones. I could see what would happen. They started throwing bigger stones, and they were having so much fun they didn't realize how they moved away from each other, how the boy with the red T-shirt had moved behind the other. They were perhaps between the ages of five and eight, and were brothers, maybe cousins. I stood up, and I was about to yell but it was too late. The boy with the red T-shirt gripped a jagged stone, a stone that barely fit in his hand, and reared back and threw it: the stone struck the other boy in the side of the head, just above his ear. The wind picked up. I couldn't hear anything, only saw his hand rise quickly to his head, the other boy turning away and hugging himself after throwing the stone, as if somehow he had been hit in the stomach. I ran over as fast as I could, my book falling to the ground, kicking over my beer. The boy screamed, blood pouring through his hands, tears streaming down his face. I took a handkerchief from my pocket, placed it against the wide-open wound; he cried out in great pain, and I had no choice but to hold him, his head against the bottom of my chest, and suddenly I was softly speaking in Spanish, No llora, no llora, don't cry, don't cry. The other boy just looked at me, and then suddenly he ran away from the shore toward the road. When I turned, the boy still in my arms, I saw a heavyset man making his way from a van, a dirty-looking gray towel in his hand. I let go of the boy, and the man held the top of his head with one hand, scrutinized the wound, and then folded the towel against it. Ponga, he said, con fuerte. He looked at me, thanked me, and they went back toward the van.

I sat back down on my chair, picked up my book, my hands wet, my white shirt soaked and ruined. My hand brushed against the open book, streaking the last page I had read—*All the yellow country and the white hills and the chaff blowing and the long lines of poplars by the road*—and I gave up and turned to the waves crashing into the stones.

I felt a hand on my shoulder. The sun had moved through its slow arc to the northwest. The blood dry on my hands, my face sore and sunburned. I heard the boys laughing. They walked, slowly, along the shore, the one boy in his red T-shirt and the other in a yellow one, a few circles of red dotting his shoulder and arm, the gray towel now wrapped around his head. I looked up toward the hand on my shoulder. The man handed me a cold beer and thanked me again. I asked him if he shouldn't take the boy to the hospital, and he shrugged a kind of *Who knows?* or an *Ay, no.* He smiled, and then turned to follow the boys running down the shore.

Sitting there on that stone-covered beach, I started to cry with abandon; almost as if I was overwhelmed by some mysterious affliction I couldn't comprehend or remember. I cried and drank the cold beer and looked at the waves. And then I remembered that a few days after Lorime had been buried, a time I hoped to forget, I went over to his house and found his father in the backyard sitting underneath a pine tree on an overturned apple crate. I came up behind him, two heavy coho salmon in my hands; I wanted to surprise him, offer him the fish and ask him if he might one day want to go fishing. When I looked over his shoulder he raised a bottle of rum to his lips, and laying on the ground between his feet was another apple crate covered with various documents and manila envelopes. There were some black-and-white photographs, and even though I knew I shouldn't look, and though I couldn't make him out for certain, I could see the remnants of Lorime in one photograph, his eyes blackened and shut, his nose blue, and his cheeks swollen and cut, and then his black hair greasy with blood. His father turned to me, tears in his eyes, and said quickly, in a cracked voice, *Not for you, Ernestito. From the lawyer, not for you.* He kicked the crate over, papers and envelopes scattering under the tree. He raised the bottle to me. *¿Por qué, Ernestito? ¿Por qué? Please, tell me why?*

I couldn't remember much of that afternoon or night after the boy had been struck with the stone. I bought a bottle of rum at some point, walked in the twilight on the path along on the edge of the sea, sipping from the bottle. The next morning I awoke in my clothes—scared, filled with fear and shame; I must've blacked out. And besides walking along the shore I only remembered my headlights following the curved road in a light fog, but then I saw the blood on my shirt, my hands, thick under my nails. I remembered the boy, stones hitting the sea. I panicked, stood up, and looked for Boogaloo; there he was, sitting on my desk, and I felt relieved, my hands shaking at my sides. I stumbled outside into the cool morning air, found my car, the top down, the inside filled with broken, wind-blown branches and blossoms, an empty rum bottle, the seats wet with dew. I turned in search of some water.

I set the glass down, licked the tears away from the side of my mouth. I looked around the table following their eyes—their openness, the clarity of concern—and I heard their voices as if I were underwater, sinking, trying to let go of the heavy stone stuck to my hand, their voices calling from above, *Everything will be okay . . . okay, everything . . .* I let go of the stone, looked straight up into the azure, sun-filled water, the waterline gold and rippled with waves, and what kept me going all of a sudden was the thought of how far the Lacasas had traveled, how my life was nothing compared to the years of struggle they had gone through, a poverty of life, a literal hunger, at times. The decisions they had painfully made in giving up their country, their family, their language; and the knowledge, perhaps, that their memories were exiled forever.

My letters to Magdalene were a memory. They seemed lost, written at times that felt so long ago, since every day I waited to hear from her and she never answered. I wondered why, what was she angry about . . . ? And then it struck me that maybe she was afraid. She and I were alike. Tentative. Shy. She was unsure of what to do. And I knew then, sitting in La Habana, that I had to go and see her mother, Ramóna. I had to prove I was no longer afraid and I needed her help—Ramóna could help me bring Magdalene and Isabel home.

I looked at Gonzalo; I imagined long, thick green rows of vines, the freshwater sea in the background, Gonzalo and Renaldo working in a small vineyard. I saw Renaldo's landscape—the blue now with green, cinnamon and cherries and grapes, his words colored by this northern place, these people who talked and ate and drank and laughed all around us.

You said you're going to make your own wine, no? I asked Gonzalo.

Absolutely. I have a Malbec vine I brought from my relatives in Argentina; it's growing in our backyard, and I think it'll continue to grow good here. I want to make a Malbec-Cabernet.

As you know, Gonzalo, there's some grapes growing out there on Mr. Johansen's property. You remember that nice open rolling field on the side of the house?

Gonzalo nodded.

If everything works out, I want you to look the field over. I want to taste wine from there some day, I said, waving my forefinger in the air.

Okay. Gonzalo stretched his hand across the table and we shook.

There was silence around the table now, broken at times by forks hitting plates, glasses being filled with ice water. I looked up at Mr. Vargas, who stood there listening, his hands clasped over his stomach, his bright white apron.

And hombre, Señor Vargas. We want to walk into this market and see bottles of Vino Lacasa here on your shelves, I told him.

Yes, yes, yes . . . Segudo, he said, licking his lips and rubbing his stomach. Everyone laughed deeply, Abuela Lacasa with her hands on her stomach, laughing at the possibility just flung into the air, circling around our ears like yellow butterflies fluttering between the branches of an avocado tree. She continued to laugh, and then when we all looked at her she was crying. Renaldo placed his arms around his father's neck, kissed him on the cheek. Julieta, standing at his side, rubbed the top of Renaldo's head. Mr. Vargas looked at me and winked.

Ay, Mamí, don't cry, Gonzalo said.

I was suddenly thinking of your father, Abuela Lacasa said, how I wish he was here. Then in my memory I heard him telling of a time in his life, laughing, remembering, and then saying, *Coño, I was so happy I almost shit my pants.* Then Abuela Lacasa let out a loud bellyful of laughter, her shoulders shivering, and said, And then I was so happy listening to you I cried.

Julieta handed Abuela a tissue.

Gonzalo said, Please, Mamí, we have a lot to be happy for, but for the love of God, don't shit your pants.

We all broke up with laughter, mine the loudest, my stomach full and warm, holding myself so my ribs would stop hurting.

Abuela Lacasa wiped her eyes, took a few deep breaths, and then said, So your daughter and her mother will come soon, right?

Yes. I know now what I need to do, and who can help me to bring them home.

Good, Ernestito, get them here quick; we'll have another party. Like this, Abuela Lacasa said, raising her arms, and then we'll laugh again, and you and Magdalene can tell me everything.

The front door opened. I saw them enter, the Johansens. I felt that since I had asked them to dinner and they were now arriving, I was beginning to do possible things.

Hey, folks, over here, I yelled, *I'm right here.*

A small change. A recognition that this was my place, and maybe these were my people.

Everyone turned to face the door.

Come on over, you're just in time.

Though it was cold on that early June morning, I started off in the dark with the top down, Boogaloo at my side. The sky was clear and bright, the pine trees dark blue shapes on the side of the highway as I made my way south. By the time I hit Grand Haven the sun was beginning to break on the horizon, and the celery and pickle fields went by first, a grayish purple, followed by the blue and green of the apple orchards, the trees full of leaves, and then the highway turned orange and gold as the morning light arose all around me. In the four-and-a-half-hour drive down to Niles, I only stopped once and peed in a clump of cattails, my only witness a blue heron who stood long and majestic on the edge of a marsh, watching as I zipped up my pants and turned back the car.

It was about nine thirty by the time I made it to Niles. I still felt a little hungover, my drunk from two nights before spilling into the dinner at La Habana the night before, and still with me this morning, my stomach nervous and my eyes straining with exhaustion. Pulling into the Swansons' driveway, their house looked quiet and empty save for the small white wooden birds that hung from their eaves on almost invisible wires, the birds turning in the morning breeze coming in from the northwest. A figure went by the picture window; when it appeared again in the kitchen, I could make out the head and shoulders—Mr. Swanson. I turned off the engine, got out, and made my way to the house.

I looked in the kitchen window: Mr. Swanson sat alone in a pair of khakis and a flannel shirt, a steaming cup of coffee to his right on the table, the front page of the paper propped up against a bowl of oranges, bananas, and mangoes. I tapped on the window. He looked up, squinted. A kind of scowl was evident on his face, but then his eyes widened with recognition, and he lifted his coffee cup from the table, blew on it, took a sip. He set it down. Looked at me again, pointed toward the front door.

Hello, Ernest. What are you doing here? I'm sure you know Magda . . .

I know Magdalene is not here; I came to see you.

Why? Mr. Swanson asked.

Well, I . . . I looked around, as if someone might walk around the corner.

Mr. Swanson put me at ease: Don't worry, Ramóna's out back working on her herb garden.

I'm sorry to arrive without calling, but do you remember that time you let me borrow some money?

Of course, I remember; you sent back more than you borrowed. Mr. Swanson stepped from inside and closed the screen door quietly. He crossed his arms against his chest.

Must've been a long drive down from up north this morning? He looked at my car.

Yes, and colder than I thought. Well, I continued, I have another favor to ask.

No problem. What is it?

I looked down at my shoes and then clasped my hands behind my back and looked him straight in the eyes.

I need to talk to Magdalene's mother. I have no one left to turn to, and I'm trying to do something . . . I don't know. Mr. Swanson was shaking his head in agreement, and so I went on:

I don't know why but Ramóna seemed like the only person I could talk to.

I'll get her, Ernest; she'll talk to you. I'll tell her Magdalene and Isabel are on the phone, and then when she comes inside you'll be here. Come on, he said waving me in with his arm, holding the door open.

It was warm inside; I didn't realize how numb my hands had been driving down. I distinctly smelled pancake batter, cinnamon and apples, maple syrup, along with strong coffee. Mr. Swanson stopped at the kitchen table, folded the newspaper in half, and then took a drink of his coffee. He turned back to me, put his hand down on the table as if he needed it to stand up.

Sit down, Ernest. Would you like a cup of coffee? He pointed toward the coffeemaker on the counter. There was a cup with a red sailboat on it and the words *Mackinac Island* in blue cursive underneath. In the kitchen window there were photographs of Isabel and Magdalene. In one they were lying back on a pile of colorful fall leaves, their smiling faces framed in bright reds and yellows, oranges tinged with greens; in another, Mr. Swanson and Ramóna were sitting at a picnic table, Isabel in Ramóna's arms and smiling into the camera, half an ear of corn in her hand, the river in the background, a long platter of cornmeal-coated fish in the middle of the table; and there was a photograph of Isabel sitting on the knee of a giant Easter bunny, a basket of colored eggs and chocolates surrounded by imitation green grass, Isabel's face enlivened by her purple dress with its white yoked collar. Mr. Swanson picked up the cup, looked at me, and shook it in the air.

Sure, I said, with a little sugar and cream.

Mr. Swanson poured me a cup of coffee, stirred in some sugar, and then the cream from a small white pitcher. He handed me the cup of coffee and stepped to the back door.

You wait here, Ernest.

I took a sip, the cream thick and sweet in my mouth, the coffee warming my insides, my eyes seeming to brighten. I held the cup tightly with both of my hands, let them begin to warm and loosen, thought of what I would say to Ramóna. I stood up and went to the window: Ramóna stood in a square of freshly spaded black dirt still wet from the morning dew, her feet wide and steady in a pair of dark green knee-high rubber boots, a hoe in her hand, and she quickly cut a small open spot into a row. She bent at the knees, the hoe resting against her thigh, and pulled an herb from a pot and placed it into the spot, patting dirt around its edges, a row of even, green plants beginning to take shape. She stood. Mr. Swanson stood behind her, watching her work, and then called her name. I turned away from the window and sat back down at the table.

Ay, Magda, finally it's you, I could hear her say as she walked through the door. She kicked off her boots, and when they struck the wall they left streaks of mud. She hurried to the phone but then stopped. She stared at me. She looked again toward the phone on the wall, the receiver still in place.

This isn't Magda. Ramóna turned back toward the door, and Mr. Swanson closed it and leaned his back against it.

No, Ramóna, it's not; she never called. He placed his coffee cup on the kitchen counter and leaned back against the door.

You see, it's Ernest, and he drove a long way this morning to talk to you.

Ramóna looked shorter in that moment without her boots, her feet covered in thick gray wool socks, her pants wrinkled from being tucked into her boots, her knees muddied. She saw me looking at her, her teeth clenching hard. She ran her hands through her hair, and when they came back to her sides they were fists, and she gently struck them together in front of her stomach. She stopped. She brought her hands up to her lips as if in prayer, and then when they moved from her lips her eyes narrowed and she said:

About what?

I don't know, Mr. Swanson said, but he said it is important.

She stared at me. What is it?

Please, you have to hear me out. I know you don't approve of me, but I have no one to turn to, and I need to talk to someone who knows Magdalene . . . I was filled with a great rush of feelings and words, and then they just stopped. Went dead. I took a sip of my coffee. This was my chance and I took it.

For the last few weeks all I did was talk to myself, walk around in memory, try to hear someone who would tell me what to do. And then I remembered that time my mother was sick, throwing up blood, and everyone thought she would die. She was in the hospital for some time, and a week must have gone by and I hadn't seen her. I know it was you, Ramóna, who called Boogaloo and asked him to take my father and me to see her.

I had to stop for a moment because my eyes welled up with tears. I took a deep breath, rocked a few times in the chair, and then tucked my hands under my arms and started again.

You let Magdalene go with me, too, even when you knew my father was really bad off—drunk every day, crying, and scared. You knew, too, that he had been fighting with my mother, that she was sick and he hit her, and that's what may have started the bleeding again.

I could see Ramóna's body shaking, and she started to cry. I had to hold my face for a moment, my mind turning from the words I wanted to say to the image of that fight, and how when they were fighting I sat there unsure of what to do, filled with a need to understand how my father could turn so angry and violent, how it was that they ever saw anything in each other—and then I almost stood up and pushed my father away. It was too late, though, the damage had been done.

I held my face with as much strength as I could; perhaps that was what I was afraid of: our pasts would always be a line of tension in our lives, a fist striking a face, and I never wanted that line to push me toward that same kind of anger or violence in front of Magdalene. I let go of my face.

You stood next to Magdalene on the sidewalk, I remember; she had a bouquet of beautiful flowers in her arms; and as you let her go you told me to make sure I kiss my mother when I see her, give her your love. You touched my arm in a way that gave me strength. It was the first time I felt there were other people connected to our lives, people who cared for us. The other day, early in the morning, I heard your voice in my memory, my arm still warm from where you had touched me, and I thought maybe you might be able to help . . .

My voice trailed off, filled with too much emotion and strain. Ramóna stepped a little closer, pulled the other chair away from the table and sat down. She crossed her arms, then uncrossed them and wiped her face.

I did that because I cared, very much so; your mother and I were close friends, and when your father ran away with you to Puerto Rico and she came back to Niles, I talked to her and helped in whatever way I could.

Ramóna cried, looking to the ceiling as if she believed that would make her stop. Her raised hands curled into fists again, and she brought them down on her thighs, the hard punch against her solid flesh filling the kitchen.

It has always been the same—you men run away, you do what you want. Now you are here, and what the hell do you want from me?

I've changed, Ramóna. I know what I want—I want Magdalene and Isabel in my life, and I'm working on buying this house and . . .

And you think your knowing you've changed, these things you've done, you think they'll make a difference?

Yes, I said. Yes, I do. I have sent her these envelopes; well, I've sent them to my father to give to her. But she's not . . .

Ramóna stood up abruptly, kicking her chair back, and she did so with such force I immediately stood up too. She walked over to the counter and opened a breadbox. She took out a loaf of bread and threw it in the sink, followed by a box of crackers and a bag of muffins. A glass broke, silverware clashed. She turned from the box with two handfuls of envelopes, maybe thirty or forty. She walked toward me.

My letters were sent back. My only daughter, what does she do but send them back, Ernest, she said, and then threw them in my face, the corner of an envelope striking me in the chest, another my hand, and another my right eye; that one stung, and my eye started blinking like crazy and tears rolled down my face. I tried to pick them up for her but she stood right in front of me and blocked my way, and then she slapped me in the face, punched me in the chest, all the while screaming, *Your letters are there coño, coño, she only sends mine back.*

Mr. Swanson tried to pull her back and hold her, but I stepped closer and told him to let her be, and when he went to push me back it was Ramóna who pushed me, and I said, Go ahead, hit me, hit me all you want. And so she hit me all at once with both hands across the chest, and then she slapped my face hard. I thought she was done but then she grabbed my hair just above my ears and brought her face close as she pulled. She let go, swayed for a moment. When it looked like she was going to fall down, I opened my arms, and the next thing I knew we were holding each other and crying. We would have fallen down if it had not been for Mr. Swanson embracing us and holding us up, his voice steady and clear, *I got you both, I got you both*, as we seemed to slowly dance around and around the same circle.

The next thing I remember was feeling so exhausted as we sat down, Mr. Swanson bringing out a cold pitcher of water and filling three tall glasses. We all took a drink. He gave Ramóna two aspirins, and then he passed two to me. I swallowed them gratefully, and he said to me:

You don't look good, Ernest.

I'm not doing too well, I said. I looked at Ramóna and told them, You might find it strange, but the hardest thing in life, regardless of what has happened in the past, is now; is living each day and trying to make decisions. For a long time I created a lonely life, and now I don't even know why. I remember being angry, filled with shame and hate . . . but that memory doesn't help me to figure out why I lived the way I did. I needed someone to turn to, and now there's no one to help me make decisions. Sometimes, I spend hours, sometimes days, filled with uneasiness and unsure of what to do. It all hit me the other day, and I did what I know might not be the best thing: I went out and got drunk.

We all laughed for a moment, cleared our throats, the tears still there. Mr. Swanson reached into a cabinet and pulled out a medicine bottle. He opened it and slid a small pink tablet across the table.

Take that, Ernest; it will help to restore the water and salt you've probably lost, and then you'll feel better, I promise.

Ramóna took a long drink of water, stretched her legs out.

I hear you, Ernestito, and I think I understand. It is not up to me to approve or disapprove, hijo, and I only told Magdalene things because I didn't want her to make the same mistakes I made. But I'm learning more about remembering mistakes, living with regret—that gets you only so far. What do you want from me?

I hesitated, looked at her a moment. She leaned forward, her elbows on her thighs.

Cuéntamelo.

I thought if you might just tell her about my coming to see you. If you just let her know I asked for your help, well, she'll understand.

I don't know, I think I might have lost her . . . Whatever I say . . .

Mr. Swanson brought over another chair, sat down next to Ramóna, and took her hand. They looked at each other and then kissed.

No, you haven't, I assured Ramóna as best I could. Magdalene's just away for a bit. She always told me that no matter what, she believed—deep down—she could turn to you, Ramóna.

Let me say something, Ernest. There were many times I could've told you what to do; I could've told you to leave Magdalene alone, to stay away from her . . . And I could've gone down to the river and told you to leave and go to your parents, go anywhere but there. I didn't. Things must change. I will do what I can, and you must do whatever it takes to make Magdalene and Isabel a part of your life. Whatever it takes. They shouldn't be alone—but, most of all, Isabel needs to know you are her father.

She stopped. She picked up her glass and took another drink of water.

But let me ask you, why don't you just go over there?

I paused, turned when I heard a robin in the backyard, remembered Boogaloo out in the car.

Let me ask *you*, why keep sending Magdalene letters, Ramóna? Why don't you go over there?

Pero—

I interrupted her: I can't go, Ramóna, because of Boogaloo, because of Manuel Perez.

Ramóna and Mr. Swanson let go of each other's hands, and for a moment they looked at each other, and then they turned to me. I could tell Ramóna wanted to say something but the words wouldn't come out. Finally, Mr. Swanson asked, What about him?

He told me a few months ago that Isabel is my daughter, but I couldn't figure out what to do, and then he died—

133

What?

He died, of a cerebral hemorrhage, up in Traverse City.

Was he visiting you? Ramóna asked.

No—well, maybe he was on his way to see me; that's the thing, I don't know what he was doing up there.

Oh, Ernest.

That's why I can't go, I told them. I want to work everything out for Magdalene and Isabel to be with me, and it would be too much right now to see my parents, to try and explain to Changó what happened.

Ramóna let out a big wail, and then she threw her head back and began to shake and cry again, *Oh my God, oh my . . .* , her wail growing into a high, mournful pitch, and then just as quickly as it started, it stopped. Her face was in her hands, down close to her knees. She lifted her head and looked at me.

Oh, Ernest, you never knew . . . never knew. Did you? She caught her breath, looked at Mr. Swanson.

Knew what?

Boogaloo.

Manuel Perez, Boogaloo, that's who I know.

No . . . no. *Ay dios*—Boogaloo is Magda's father.

I had no words. My mouth went dry. I had often forgotten to consider Boogaloo in that way, as a father. Yet even though there were plenty of times I hated Boogaloo, those times were distant and vague, and what made Boogaloo distinct in my memory were his moments of tender generosity. I remembered what he had said: *If I could do it all over again, I'd do anything to know my daughter.*

Maybe Boogaloo was coming to visit me so he could tell me about Magdalene, I said. Maybe he was going to tell me to bring her home—but I can't go there now.

There was a wave of silence between us, the kitchen filling with strong warm light as the sun moved west and came in through the window. Mr. Swanson bent over, pulled one of his socks up, and then ran his thumb and forefinger down the crease of his khakis. He crossed his right leg over his left and took Ramóna's hand in his own.

You won't have to go, he said; we'll go and tell Magdalene everything. We'll get her to come back home.

Ramóna pulled her hand away, raised it to her mouth, and looked at Mr. Swanson with astonishment.

But how, how can we ever do that?

We can. We just can, Mr. Swanson said, his eyes small and serious, no room for doubt at all in his face.

Ramóna took his hand again and held it close to her cheek for a moment, her eyes closed. She opened her eyes. Mr. Swanson opened her hand, raised her palm to his lips and kissed it.

We can do it . . . We must, Ramóna.

That's right; we can—we need Magdalene to know she's wanted here, that she's loved. And I've needed to go back for a long time, she said, turning toward me and smiling as best she could.

I took a long, slow drink of water, finishing off the glass. I poured another quarter of a glass and drank it down. The deep pocket of my stomach felt hard and strong, and I felt the best I had in a long time, and though my legs were tired, I was ready to drive back and do what I needed to do to prepare for Magdalene and Isabel's arrival. I stood and stretched, and they stood too.

Thank you, thank you for everything.

I moved closer and opened my arms, giving Ramóna a long hug, and she rubbed my back and gave me a small kiss on the cheek. I turned to Mr. Swanson and shook his hand.

I've taken enough of your time today, but thanks again for talking with me. I've got a long drive back, and a lot to do tomorrow.

So, Ernestito, Ramóna asked, you have a house you are buying?

Yes. Tomorrow I meet the owner to see if everything's all set to buy it. It's so nice and . . .

Ramóna stopped me, pointing to the clock. She said, Sit down, Ernest; we want to hear all about the house. She looked at Mr. Swanson, held his eyes for a moment, and then she turned to me and said:

It's late, and you do look tired, hijo. You stay here tonight, on the couch, and we'll wake you up early so you can make it home in plenty of time.

I sat back down and shook my head.

And for now you tell us the whole story, and when we see Magdalene we can share it with her, tell her how you were not afraid to come and ask us for help, and she'll see why it's time for her to come home.

We were to meet at six and I wanted to make sure I didn't arrive too early, or too late, so I drove out to Mr. Johansen's at ten minutes to six. I pulled in past the front gate, turned into the field, and shut off the engine. Walking down the dirt lane next to the field toward the cottage, I could see Mr. Johansen down the lane, his truck parked under the front birch trees, as he lifted pieces of plywood into the truck bed. He waved; I waved back.

I hope I'm not late?

Not at all—I just finished opening all the windows. Now standing on the front porch, Mr. Johansen waved for me to follow him inside.

The sunlight fell through the northwest windows, filled with dust motes. The floors were wood, honey colored, and shiny in the sun. The front room wide and deep, with a small fieldstone fireplace next to the northwest windows, a pile of wood ready to be burned. Mr. Johansen walked through the doorway into the kitchen, turning on the light. The refrigerator door was open. I stepped into the doorway.

I'm going to run upstairs.

Go ahead.

I went back through the front room and took the stairs two at a time. The back bedroom, this will be for Isabel. I walked in. There was a small skylight overhead, a window looking out onto a lone pine, and then in the distance, blue: the curling waves, the freshwater sea seeming to lift white blossoms toward the sky. I turned and left the room, crossed the hallway into the large front bedroom. It had two skylights and two windows facing the southwest. For Magdalene, the window on the right, with a small table, the view of the row of birch trees out front shaking in the wind, their little leaves glinting with the last of the evening sun.

Back downstairs, Mr. Johansen stood in the back doorway.

I had the lights turned on yesterday, and the propane tanks filled. I'd clean the refrigerator out real good if I were you, before I'd plug it in, he said, pointing to the open door.

I nodded.

How's the upstairs?

Perfect. I stood in the doorway between the front room and the kitchen, my forearm held shoulder height, leaning against the doorway. Mr. Johansen eyed a piece of white paper folded on the counter next to the sink. Our eyes met.

Check that figure I've written down, Ernest, and if the price is agreeable, then it's fine by the bank and me.

I dropped my arm, stepped to the counter. I picked up the piece of paper. On the day I had picked up Boogaloo's ashes I had brought him out here to look at the cottage with me. Once I arrived, with Boogaloo at my side, I suddenly felt bold and crossed over the fence, made my way closer than I had ever done before. I sat down in the field and looked up at the cottage every so often while reading a book, Boogaloo sitting next to me. I never heard Mr. Johansen drive up; I had fallen asleep, the book open across my chest, Boogaloo inside the crook of my arm. When Mr. Johansen shook me awake, I jumped up. Mr. Johansen told me, *Hold on, hold on there*, as I stumbled around holding on to Boogaloo and beginning to run. He held my shoulder for a moment. He said he'd seen my car parked by the fence quite a few times over the last six months. Before he could say anything else I quickly apologized for being on his property, told him I had meant no harm, especially for falling asleep. I told him, I think it's a beautiful cottage, and then extended my hand and introduced myself. He bent over, picked up my book, read the spine, smiled, and then handed it to me. We walked along the edge of the field, my book tucked under one arm, Boogaloo tucked under the other. We talked about the weather and the property, and Mr. Johansen then asked me what I did for a living and how I liked living up here. When I said good-bye, Mr. Johansen told me to stop by anytime, and that if I walked the lane past the cottage I'd enter a field that went down to the lake. He added that I might enjoy reading my book down on the beach.

I unfolded the white piece of paper.

After that first meeting, we met out in the field often, walking and talking; and one night I ran into Mr. and Mrs. Johansen coming out of La Habana with a small bag of groceries. I had asked them if they had ever eaten dinner there; they hadn't. I asked them to join me, shaking a small box; I wanted to share with them the pasteles my family had just sent from Puerto Rico, which I knew Mr. Vargas would warm up and add to our dinners. They accepted the invitation. I felt by the time we finished eating that they knew a good deal about my life. Then one Saturday I drove by the property and saw Mr. Johansen cutting some wood on the edge of the field. I stopped, threw my suit coat on the backseat, rolled up my sleeves. That Saturday I helped Mr. Johansen deep into the evening. We finally stopped only, it seemed, because Mrs. Johansen arrived with some fried chicken, a bowl of red potatoes boiled with vinegar and salted, warm bread, and a couple of cold beers. Feeling full, loose, and happy with the physical labor, the food, and the company, I asked, You folks ever think about selling the cottage? Finally, last week Mr. Johansen had called and told me to go see his banker, and if everything worked out with the banker, I could buy the cottage.

Yes, Mr. Johansen, this is more than agreeable. *It's a dream.*

Good to hear. On Monday, at four o'clock, we'll meet at the bank to sign the paperwork.

I'll be there. And thank you—this is all so . . . generous, and I truly appreciate it, Mr. Johansen.

Mr. Johansen closed the back door, turning the kitchen light off.

Not to worry, Ernest. You're buying it, and it will be good to have you next door.

We walked back through the front room onto the porch and then down the steps into the front yard. Mr. Johansen turned to me. We shook hands.

You'll have a lot of cleaning to do before your daughter and her mother arrive. Remember, we're just on the other side of the field; if you need anything, give us a call.

Thanks again, thank you for everything.

Mr. Johansen walked to his truck, opened the door. He smiled and waved.

I lifted my arm; it felt just on the edge of numbness, and without weight, as I waved. I watched Mr. Johansen cross the field and then his taillights disappeared when he turned into the dark trees.

Some might have said the cottage was a home for ghosts. There was some tragedy that had happened in Mr. Johansen's life; he had boarded up the cottage. But he never said why, and I never asked, though I heard from a local winemaker that Mr. Johansen could gauge a person almost immediately. For some reason he liked me, and he felt I should live in the cottage. Mr. Johansen wanted to begin living without denying his past—that, I decided, was the reason for his kindness.

I turned and looked down the long field that led to the lake: now a dark blue shadow I could barely see. I began to cross the field. This visit was the closest I had ever been to the cottage, my first time inside; the cottage's windows were all the more spectacular with the plywood taken down.

You'll have a lot of cleaning to do before your daughter and her mother arrive.

For the first time in my life—here, standing in the field, the tall grass swaying around me, and in the distance the sea roaring into the stony shore—I had no fear or indecision: I knew Magdalene and Isabel would arrive soon. When my father took me away and we were gone from my mother for a long time, I walked into my abuela's kitchen one day and found Boogaloo reading a letter. He told Changó that my mother needed for him to bring me home. She wanted Changó to come home, too. My father looked at the letter, tried to make sense of the words. He was weeping, asking, *She said this?* then said, *Don't lie to me, that is what she wants . . . ?*

I could see Magdalene finally reading my letters, perhaps now less afraid, like me, knowing she needed to bring Isabel home. I could see the family sitting around a table under a mango tree, eating dinner, Ramóna and Mr. Swanson sitting across from Isabel and Magdalene, and I could see how Ramóna was helping me, how she was telling Magdalene about how I had asked for help, and about this cottage and how we had a chance to start our lives without shame, hate, or fear. Love, she might even say, is ours.

Two swallows rose from the tall grass, swerved in front of me, the arc of their flight spreading across the dark sky. There was sand and stones just ahead, and then the freshwater sea sounding loud and clear and clean.

When Magdalene arrives, I'll bring her and Isabel to the cottage, their cottage. I'll show them around; show Isabel her room, show Magdalene the table I've set up for her in front of her window. Then we'll go downstairs and walk through this field, and I'll tell her all I know of her father's life, his death.

I started toward my car. I stopped, turning back to the sea. When I picked up Boogaloo's ashes they gave me his wallet, a ring of keys, and a small glass box with little pieces of colored paper collaged into the glass; and when I raised the lid I found there was a mirror at the bottom. I had to share these things with Magdalene, too. I'd take her to St. Joe and we'd discover what locks the keys opened, and for some reason I had this sure feeling that the glass box was for her. I'd let her open it, and when she saw her face—that flawless and beautiful face—I hoped she'd have the same feeling of sureness.

I suddenly remembered her face, wet with the river, the first time I was struck by how beautiful and precious it was. One fall day, when I stepped out of the cabin, the air was filled with the most awful stench. The worms—I suddenly sensed—in the odor of decay and earth, the worms—it must be the worms. That past June, under a mulberry tree, in a soft square of earth near the riverbank, I had dug a hole and placed the steel of an old wheelbarrow in the ground for my worms. When I turned the top layer with my boot, all I saw were bloated and mushy worms, their bodies broken and torn from within. I gagged, closed my eyes, and turned away. From the side of the cabin I brought a five-gallon bucket and a shovel. I filled the bucket with dirt and worms, and then walked over to the river and flung the mess as far as I could. It was the last Saturday of September, the afternoon warm. The sun was bright and beginning to descend when I saw Magdalene's dark figure outlined in gold, my eyes stinging with sweat from the shoveling. I wiped my brow and shielded my eyes. Magdalene was wearing a pair of khaki shorts and a white tank top, a hooded sweatshirt over her arm. Her mocha hair—brilliant in the sun with shades of coffee—was pulled back with a yellow ribbon, her ponytail laying flat against her chest. Magdalene's skin soft and smooth—lovely, browned from the summer months, and glowing next to her white tank top, her yellow ribbon, her bright almond-shaped eyes.

She smiled briefly, her lips turning to a frown. She put down the picnic basket she was carrying. She placed her hands on her hips.

Ernestito, *what's that smell?* Her eyebrows raised and her eyes widened, and she pinched her nose.

We both laughed. I spit, and then lifted another shovelful of dirt and worms in the bucket, lifted it, and flung them in the river, the dirt splashing like a hard rain, the dead worms disappearing in the golden-brown currents.

I struck the shovel on the edge of the sunken wheelbarrow and pried at it; it barely budged. I lifted the shovel and struck down again, feeling Magdalene at my side. We both pulled down on the shovel handle, once, twice, and then grunted on the third try, the earth giving way, the steel loosening and rising from the dirt. We bent down and grabbed the edge of the wheelbarrow, and then we lifted it and started toward the river. A hot, prickling sensation of pain started immediately along my legs and arms, my neck, and then the edges of my ears. I heard Magdalene yell, *Ouchy, ouchy,* and then, *Coño, Ernestito.* We started running toward the river, the wheelbarrow still in our hands, and I could see bees swarming all around my head—somehow they were there, nesting in that soft dirt under the mulberry tree, and Magdalene and I had released them into a swarming fury. We dove in with a loud splash, letting the wheelbarrow fall into the currents. The river was fast and strong and cold, and I held myself under the sun-tinted water, the water numbing all the bee stings. I watched as Magdalene's legs kicked away from me. I went down and touched the bottom, held on to a stone, and then let go and rose to the surface, gasping, and took a deep breath. I called for Magda.

She was there, calmly floating on the river, circling in the small pool in front of the cabin, her arms like slow windmills digging deep into the water. I stood, the water just to my chest. Magdalene turned over, smiled, and then dove deep and came toward me. She pulled on my waist, and when I went to grab her I was too late; she was suddenly gone, and then I heard water splashing and turned: Magdalene stood on the shore, pulling her hair back and twisting water from it, her shorts and tank top tight and dripping with water against her body.

Bees still swarmed around the gaping hole in the ground, though they seemed crazy and erratic, weak in the late September air. My arms burned with stings, my neck felt swollen, and my ears were numb. Magdalene's face looked so clean and brown and beautiful even though she was covered with red welts.

We'd better take off our clothes, she said; and as I watched her kick off her sneakers, unbutton her shorts, and slide them over her hips and down her legs, I kicked off my boots and pulled down my jeans. When I lifted

141

my shirt over my head, I saw Magdalene's yellow ribbon tangled around her neck. I reached toward her.

Here, Magda, turn around.

Her back was smooth, her dark hair hanging in thick, wet curls just above her shoulder blades. I lifted her hair and squeezed, water running down her back; she shivered, turned to me briefly, our eyes meeting for a moment before she looked to the ground. Gathering her hair at the back of her neck, I wrapped the yellow ribbon around her hair twice, and then tied a double knot.

Stand still, I said, and did the only thing I could think to do. With my hands I lifted soft mud from the shore to her shoulders, slowly rubbing it along her back and arms. I let the mud thicken and spread, my hands softly and gently following the curves of her body, down the small of her back, and along the rise of her buttocks, Magdalene's warmth pulsing through my hands, coursing its way down into the deep pocket of my stomach.

It feels better, cooler already, she said.

I turned her around and dabbed mud on her forehead and cheeks, across the welts beginning to rise more profusely in a chaotic pattern. When I looked at her breasts they were wet and red, her nipples pressing hard against the fabric of her bra. She held my hands to her and cupped them around her breasts, and I looked into her hazel eyes; a small tear fell from her right eye, and then she blinked, smiled, and kissed me on the lips. My hands fell to my sides. She unclasped her bra and it fell to the ground.

More, Ernest, please.

I lifted more mud and spread it over the top of her shoulders, following the curve of her breast down along the flatness of her taut stomach. Magdalene was the only girl I had ever been around—we were friends since forever. But with her so close to me, on that September day, my eyes and hands discovering all the shapes of her flesh, I felt like my heart had stopped; my hands began to tremble, and, standing there in my wet underwear, Magdalene must have seen my desire for her.

I bent over and raised a handful of mud to my face, and then another for my shoulders, my chest, down my arms, the mud cool against the stinging and swelling that I couldn't control.

Ernest, turn around, she told me.

Facing the river, I felt Magdalene step up behind me. She wrapped her arms around my chest, her breasts against my back, her thighs soft against the back of my thighs. She trembled and held me tighter; I felt the side of her face rubbing my shoulder, and she kissed the back of my neck, and as I watched the brown river flowing on with the glint of the golden sun, I started to shake and tremble, too, until together we found we could sway to the touch of our skins, our skins marked by water and mud, the sting of the bees beginning to change the shape of our hearts.

We must've been seventeen then, and I'm certain we both felt the power of Magdalene's mother's dream: that Magdalene would go away to college.

But I had another sure feeling—and somehow that afternoon stayed with me, regardless of Magdalene's going away, and somehow that moment helped to bring me to this very moment. Here, in the darkening blues of the evening, the memory of those welts rising along the back of my neck, my stomach and thighs awash with desire.

I broke off a handful of the long grass. I held my closed fist in the air, then let go and watched the pieces drift off into the blues of the evening. My heart rose in my chest, and I had this feeling as if there was some heavy burden lifting from my shoulders. *One day, Magdalene, whenever you're ready, you, Isabel, and I will stand in this same spot, and, if you want, we'll scatter your father's ashes and plant his memory forever between this field and this sea. We'll plant Boogaloo's memory in the middle of our lives, and on a warm sunny day, with the fragrance of flowers and honey, stones and sea, we'll see bees and feel your father's presence close to the earth, a deep song there where we stand.*

Looking farther out into the blues of the evening, listening to the bellow of a tanker's horn from the dark waters of the sea, I started to tremble and sweat, and then when I started to laugh inside, I knew some sense of joy was tied to staying close to the earth, and I knew our time here was meant for us to hear the song we needed to hear to keep us even closer.

Part Four

Magdalene

The sweat between her breasts began to cool. She pulled on the shoulders of her T-shirt, releasing the moisture. Abuelo and Lillo lifted a sheet of corrugated tin on the roof, the sheet scraping the tops of the blocks as they slid it across. Dusk was beginning to rise from the red clay compound. Lillo's arms gleamed with sweat; he heaved the tin, giving it one final shove, and then let it drop flat across the top. Lillo and Abuelo raised their hats, cement dust powdering the air, and they both looked at the temporary roof they had created in case it rained tonight.

She could now see more of its form: the block house they were building on this mountain for Abuela and Abuelo was taking shape, two more walls finished today, as well as a small stall for a shower and a stool. Lillo climbed the ladder, a block in each hand. When he reached the final rung he leaned over, laying the blocks on the tin. The sun shifted to the west, the mountains darkening, the sky streaked with bright orange light. Magdalene lifted a cement bucket and heaved it hard toward the bushes: the water left the bucket silver, caught in the orange light for a moment, splashed green in the bushes, and then turned dark red when it fell to the dirt. She stacked together all the buckets she had rinsed, took them in her arms, and walked across the compound; she set them around the corner of a newly completed wall, under the tin roof. The cement smelled soft and wet, a cool sensation rising up her arms.

Lillo jumped off the ladder. He brushed his straw hat against his thigh, his white hair molded to his head like a just-shaped snow cone. He set his hat on the bottom rung of the ladder, lifting a machete.

Ernest's mother walked by—clean yellow cloths cradled in her arms—limping, the cast on her right leg covered in red dust. Magdalene brushed her hands together and stepped forward to help her.

A hand grasped her shoulder.

Enough work for the day, no? Changó asked. Don't worry, Magda, she'll be okay.

Two weeks ago, helping Changó clear some brush, Evelyn tripped and fell down an incline, breaking her ankle. In moments like this, the bright yellow cloths still coloring her memory, understanding the quiet, mutual ways Evelyn and Changó made a life for each other, Magdalene felt the endurance of love, how love can survive beyond fate or memory. There was something beyond the pain of the past, and something as immediate and real as the orange light Changó stood in while he looked at his wife. He nodded, yelling to Evelyn, Don't worry, I'll take care of my eye, his right eye covered with a white patch, two strips of tape holding it down.

Please hold this, Magda. Changó handed Magdalene a roll of surgical tape, and she slipped it into the back pocket of her shorts.

Lillo walked over and handed Changó the machete. Changó looked toward the jungle, waved the machete, and motioned for Magdalene to follow. She took a quick step to catch up with him, took his hand, and then walked across the compound, smoke drifting in front of them. Isabel waved, a banana leaf in her hand. Evelyn unfurled a tablecloth in the breeze, smoothing the top of the table in yellow. Abuela, wearing a red cloth over her head like a pirate, stood in front of her brick stove. She and Isabel fanned away smoke with banana leaves, waiting for the kindling to catch fire. She had all her pots ready to go, and Magdalene could smell the pungent aroma of black pepper, oregano, salt, garlic, and olive oil—all crushed and mixed in the mortar—and the peeled bananas and cut-up pieces of yuca for the goat stew she was making.

Magdalene waved back to Isabel. The child was becoming more and more attached to Abuela and Evelyn; and Magdalene hoped when they left it wouldn't be too hard on her—or them.

Changó stopped, squeezed her hand. They were standing in front of a thick line of trees. He pointed to a worn red path and she followed behind. The jungle came on suddenly—from Isabel's voice, to silence, to a deeper silence of green in just a few steps, as if when they took another step they would be swallowed. They were descending a steep incline, and as Changó swiped the machete just before his steps, leaves and branches falling away, a thin red trail revealed itself.

I want to show you, he said, pointing the machete deeper down the trail, pointing to a slope of dark dirt giving way to a blackish green hole.

They stood under a grove of trees, some with high, thin branches and silvery leaves, others with thick, black branches, like tails or whips glittering with pink and red leaves. She hugged herself; it was much cooler here, her teeth all of a sudden chattering, a swirl of cold air drifting up in a wide stream from within the dark slope.

She fought off a shiver. Show me the way, she told him.

Changó laughed, his teeth chattering loudly. His shoulders trembled. He lifted the machete and with his other hand held one of the thin branches. He sliced off the tail and handed it to her. The bark was rough and hard, the thin whip of wood light, easily bending in her hands.

Changó drove the machete into the ground, just off the trail.

You can take pieces and make baskets—all kinds, he told her—squared, short, circled, long. He bent imaginary branches into different shapes with his hands and arms. People have made them for a long time.

A trio of hummingbirds circled them, the air green with their wings, the air they stirred whirring in Magdalene's ears.

Changó seemed to follow them deeper into the green; he grabbed his machete and told her to watch her step. Tentatively she followed, watching his back, his light blue shirt speckled with sweat and red dust, then focused on her feet. There was nothing to hold on to, and she tried to step lightly, as if she could keep part of her weight off the ground. She turned sideways, stepping one foot after another, side by side. She heard Isabel yell in the distance. The trees stirred above them, Isabel's voice lost in the moving leaves, the branches rubbing and whipping together. The trail continued to sink in front of her; she smelled wet dirt, fallen leaves, the tart smell of some fruit she could not name. She slipped, her hands breaking her fall, and slid down the trail, her hands wet with dirt, leaves, small pebbles, and stones.

Changó stood on the edge of a small pool, his pants rolled up to his knees.

She raised herself up. Silver light squeezed through the canopy of leaves. Breathless, Magdalene reached for her chest, her heart, breathed deeply. The ground steamed in spots with thin ghosts of dancing air.

How do you say? Changó stopped, the tips of his fingers inching from his mouth as he searched for the word. A sinking? he asked.

He stood on the edge of a small, clear pool surrounded by tall black stones.

This starts a stream that runs all the way to the sea, Changó told her, pointing from the pool out into the darkening trees.

She asked, You call it a sinkhole, no? We are down in a sinkhole?

Yes, yes. That's what I wanted to tell you. They are everywhere around here. He raised his arms, spun his torso in a short arc.

Look, he said, pointing at the pool.

There were small ripples, and Magdalene could see underneath the circling water. She bent closer. Little pink starlike figures darted around in the pool. Then they straightened out and became recognizable: tiny, almost transparent shrimps.

Los abahõs, Changó said.

The underneaths, she thought. *The down belows, those down here. These that become down here, underground, in hidden streams, before there can ever be a sea.*

Changó clasped his hands in front of his waist. He looked solemn. His eye patch drooped off his eye, his eyelid red. He seemed almost upset in his quietness, staring at the pool without moving. She slipped off her sandals and stepped into the pool, reached out, and touched his forearm.

It's lovely here. I've never seen anything like this.

He looked at her, took her hand, and raised it to his mouth, kissing her palm.

I wanted you to see it before you leave, Magda.

She followed his eyes into the trees, the high leaves, and in the small open spaces between leaves, the clear, darkening sky beginning to take on light, the sudden sight of a cluster of stars becoming the abahõs for her.

One day I want Ernest to see this water, Changó said.

The trees were wild with birds. They looked at each other. She raised her voice:

Don't ever think, Changó, if you don't hear from him, or see him, Ernest doesn't know there's much you can show him.

She looked away from him, down into the pool, startled by her own voice. The pool was now deepening with the darkness rising around them. She remembered the cool blue shadow she wanted to envelop her long ago; it was here with her again, along with her desire to see Ernest in this pool.

You know . . . She lost the words. Caught her breath. She wouldn't cry here. She closed her fists, her face suddenly flushed. She told Changó:

There are so many times I want to talk to him, too—she stopped, the strong, startling voice she had heard coming from herself earlier gone. The water was cold, smooth around her ankles, and it glittered with the pink abahõs swimming around her feet. *I wonder what he's doing, where he's at, if now, at this very moment, he's looking out onto the lake, a gold field darkening in the evening, yet still brilliant with the day's sun?*

She told Changó, *Ernest knows, he thinks of you.*

He shook his head and sat down, his feet still in the water. He bent forward, lifted water to his face, his left eye.

But listen . . . She sat down.

Changó looked up, water running down the left side of his face, onto his chest. She pulled the drooping patch away from his right eye. She bent forward and cupped water to the top of his head, let it run down both eyes. She repeated the gesture.

Ay, that feels good.

Listen . . .

Changó straightened himself.

Maybe you can bring Isabel and let her see this water?

He didn't respond.

I hope you will, you are her abuelo. You could show her, and she would never forget.

Changó reached over and took her hands. They both stood, and he squeezed her hands tighter, looking straight into her eyes.

Yes, I can bring Isabel, and maybe she can tell her father.

Isabel can, she can tell Ernest. She will remember and tell her father.

Mamí . . . Changólito . . .

Changó whistled back.

Come back. Hurry up—we wanna go, she yelled from up above.

Wind burst through the trees, Magdalene's hair twisting in her eyes. The birds noisily stirred again. She pulled her hair away from her face.

Changó said, Ernest wouldn't have told you, I guess?

What? Magdalene asked.

He did see this place—a place like it, once.

He did?

I took him when he was little. Up on another mountain, by Abuela's home in Rincon. So many days he would look up at the mountain, see people slowly walking up to the top—you could see their white or red shirts in the green. Ernestito asked, almost every day, if we could go too.

Changó put his hands on his knees, looking into the pool.

So you took him up the mountain? Magdalene asked, trying to get him back there, helping Changó begin again.

Maybe, maybe halfway. We didn't need to go all the way because I wanted him to see a place, the place where the stream in the mountain began for the sea. A place where I swam when I was a boy.

The wind shook the trees again. A small yellow bird landed on a rock on the edge of the pool, pecked at the water a few times, and then darted away like a darkening shadow let loose in the wind.

Changó said, Where the water fell from the side of the mountain, we placed a long banana leaf, and a small shower came down. There were rocks and stones like these, he said, raising his hands, and the water made a pool, maybe three or four feet wide and few feet deep. I took Ernest there, and we spent the afternoon swimming. We only left, I think, because the sky turned dark blue and filled with bats.

Magdalene listened closely to the water around them, listened to Changó, and tried to see how this twilight was made of the same color and density he was describing, filled with the same sounds shaped by water and stone. She heard the pool filling with a trickle, then the stream curving and falling through rocks. The wind up above them seemed to hold water and flow through the leaves in a torrent. When the wind stopped, she heard birds, the leaves still slightly stirring, the stream, and once she let those sounds fall away, Magdalene heard the sea's surf booming into the sand. She lifted her feet from the pool and let the water trickle slowly from her feet; she heard that night on the stone beach, felt Ernest's hand on the small of her back, and how she rose from and fell into him with the rhythm of the waves striking against stones. Goosebumps rose along her thighs and arms. She blushed, and then held her face for a moment. It was impossible, she knew, but she felt how strong the earth is when we listen to all the water coursing below us in an endless rush of pools, streams, and rivers flowing into a great sea.

Changó?

Yes, Magda.

Ernest has lived forever by water—you know that, right?

Ah, that's true, Changó said. I haven't seen him in so long. But always, I guess, always he has lived listening to water.

Changó, I've always wanted to ask you something.

Go ahead.

Why did my mother always seem to dislike you so much?

Ah, you make it sound much nicer than it is; I think she hates me.

They both smiled. Changó laughed.

I don't know, Magda. I've sometimes wondered myself . . . You know, we were friends long ago, when we were children. But then I went to work. My father sent me to the fields. I left the island when I turned sixteen, and I didn't see your mother again until I was about twenty or so. We both showed up in New York for a call for workers wanted in Niles, to work at Green Giant. They called our names, and we immediately recognized each other.

Changó paused, scratching the back of his neck. We were strangers by then, no matter how much we recognized each other, and I can think of no reason why she was mad at me. We both went to Niles, but we never talked.

She shook her head, shrugged her shoulders.

Do you know who my father is?

Have you asked your mother?

I have asked her, I've asked many times. She would never tell me; she still won't.

I won't come between you and your mother, Magda. But you are old enough to know. If Isabel is my granddaughter . . . Well, to hell with it. He raised his hand, his forefinger stirring the air.

Manuel Perez. Manuel is your father. Boogaloo.

Boogaloo . . . Boogaloo, she said, as if it was all clear, except that what became clearest was how hollow she felt inside, her arms filled with some odd shooting pain, and then she closed her hands into tight fists, angry at her mother, angry for how much of her memory she would never share with her. Magdalene knew nothing of Boogaloo, Manuel Perez. He had worked with Changó and Ernest in the fields, but she couldn't remember him in Niles. She lifted her right foot from the pool, listened again to the dripping water, then lowered it back down into the cold. She blinked and released a memory: a summer day. The only time she remembered her family and Ernest's family getting together. She and Ernest must have been about eleven or twelve then. She saw Ernest and Evelyn and Changó sitting at a picnic table with a big bowl of rice and a pot of red beans, an octopus salad, and a pitcher of iced tea laid out in front of them.

A picnic at Island Park. There was a thin man standing next to the grill, holding a pair of tongs. His wavy black hair brushed off his brow, his skin very dark, and she remembered now that he had on an elegant guyabera and an exquisite purple scarf tied around his neck. He was quite striking standing there—his high, hard checkbones and the whitest of teeth, a gentle smile. It was an odd moment; no one spoke, and the wind lightly rustled the mulberry trees, and she heard berries splashing into the river. Her mother had her arm around her shoulder protectively, and it was her stepfather who took her hand and said, Magdalene, we'd like for you to meet Manuel Perez.

Manuel said hello to them, shook her stepfather's hand. He went to the table and lifted what he called El Guaracha del Mundo, the Song of the World—two delicate, almost crystal-clear pink and white seashells that, he said, came from the waters near Loíza. He gave one each to Magdalene and Ernest, and then told them to hold them to their ears. The sound was deafening, a loud roar at first, and she and Ernest jerked the shells from their ears, their eyes wide. Then she slowly raised the shell back to her ear and looked at her mother; she seemed so sad, filled with some kind of fear, her eyes dark and tense. Magdalene blinked, tried to shout out her mother's eyes, and then her ears took in more and more of the shell's music, the loud roaring of the sea becoming a pulsing, then diminishing, back-and-forth rhythm, the sound of water and sand, sea birds, trees shaking in the wind, a lonely guitar, and, every now and then, the briefest of silences: a fragile region where Magdalene could place her own unbetrayed sounds.

Manuel said he was happy to meet them all. Everyone else on that day knew him though; she thought he must've been happy on that day to finally meet her, his daughter. He turned the pork chops over on the grill, a stream of smoke rising up for a moment, followed by loud sizzling sounds. He handed Changó the tongs. He bent over a cooler and pulled out a bottle of rum. Changó told him, You don't have to go, Boogaloo. He shrugged a kind of quizzical, What's one to do? He said, Maybe another day, and then he walked through the mulberry trees, the bottle glinting with coldness at his side.

She remembered how odd it was that not more than a minute later her mother said, We should go now, and she briefly pulled at her hair as if it hurt or was tangled. You haven't eaten yet, Ernest's mother said, and everyone looked at Magdalene's mother, even her stepfather. Then her stepfather asked Ernest's parents if they could bring Magdalene home later. Magdalene's mother looked at Changó with angry eyes and started to object, but then her stepfather put his arm around her, hugging her tightly. Let's go, he said, she'll be fine, don't worry, turning her away.

She thought of how Changó had said, You don't have to go, Boogaloo, and she was filled with anger again because her father did not stop, did not stay, and he seemed almost defeated in his silent loneliness as he walked away. Nobody was strong on that day—all of them knew, except for Ernest and herself, but they were all afraid, they were all filled with fear—just like me, she said to herself, trying to fill the hollowed pain welling up from her stomach into her chest.

Thank you, Changó; I've always wanted to know. Don't worry, you can't come between my mother and me; she created a distance between us long ago that I've learned to live with.

Changó nodded.

I know she loves Isabel; and she knows Ernest is Isabel's father, but . . . But, she thought, *who am I to judge—look at me, away from Isabel's father, afraid to tell Isabel or Ernest.*

Don't forget, Magda: Ramóna loves you very much, too.

She nodded, knowing there was some truth to Changó's words; deep down, her mother loved her, yet her love was something Magdalene would have to come to terms with over time, or simply let go of so she could go on. She pulled the roll of surgical tape from her pocket, held it in her mouth. She flattened the gauze eye patch against her palm, then remembered: somewhere in her old bedroom, at her mother's house, she still had that shell, El Guaracha del Mundo.

Is your eye dry? she asked, her teeth biting down on a piece of tape.

Changó raised his hand to his eye, tentatively rubbing his eyelid.

I believe yes.

Let's put this back on, then, before we go back. Changó turned to her, and as he felt her place the patch over his eye, he raised his hand to hold it in place.

Can I ask you one more question?

Segudo.

She placed a strip of tape over his eye, from his forehead to his cheek, and then added one more strip, so that there were train tracks across his eye.

How do you remember Manuel . . . Boogaloo? she asked him.

Well, I remember him as Boogaloo, a good man. When he was young he was an honest, hard worker. He could be cruel, mean with a joke or some harsh words; some people will remember him in this way. But this was only one side, and maybe just his way to fight when he was sad or angry. Whenever I wasn't sure where my life was going, why I was even sometimes living, Boogaloo was there. He was the one who helped me get sober. And for no other reason than because he had respect for life. We were distant cousins and best of friends.

This is good to know.

Yes; and you know, the last time I saw your father he was doing well, living alone in Chicago, working as a cook.

My father . . . Well? As a cook? Alone?

You have to understand, he hadn't drunk in a long time, and he looked healthy and happy—almost ten years younger than the last time I saw him. He lived in a little one-room apartment, right next to the El, and I remember how clean and shiny the wooden floors were. He sat on a folding chair in the sunlight, strips of light falling through the blinds, and when the train rumbled overhead passing by, he leaned back a little, turned his head, and just seemed to listen to something very important. Changó stopped, pushing on the patch over his eye.

My father, she said to herself, and it sounded real to connect the words with a person, a living memory; and to now see how there were things that might survive outside her memory.

She asked, My father knows of me, right?

Yes. There were many years when he didn't; he came back to Puerto Rico for a time, not knowing your mother was pregnant. And he only left in the first place because he'd been hurt. He was deeply in love with your mother—they dated for five or six months. But one day after he had gone away into one of his weeks of drink, she told him that she never wanted to see him again. The next time he saw your mother she was married to your stepfather, and you were nine or ten years old. I don't know how it was that he came to ask your mother about you; he told me once that as soon as he saw you walking with your mother, he instantly recognized something of himself in your face, the way you held your hands at your side.

Changó folded his hands on his stomach. He looked at Magdalene and said:

Yes, he knew of you, Magda. On that last day I saw him in Chicago, he was quiet. I remember there was one shelf tacked to the wall, and on the shelf he had a few seashells, a couple of books, on cooking, I believe. And there was a glass box with small pieces of color in the glass, and Boogaloo held it in his palm and opened the box so I could see the mirror in the bottom. He said that if you ever found him he wanted to give it to you, so you could see yourself, so you could remember your face, how brown and beautiful—and, for him, always perfect.

She started to cry and raised her hands to her face, quickly wiping her eyes with her palms. She said:

I always knew my father was Puerto Rican; my mother always reminded me when she was angry—and, when she was really angry, she said I had a face of dirt, cada suciedad. Magdalene thought of how confusing that always was—*a face of dirt is a dirty face. Why would my mother need to be so mean? What did she not want me to see? And how did she think I would see myself in the future with those words to guide me?*

Why didn't he ever come see me? she asked.

Because when he was finally convinced he should confront your mother, you were almost twelve years old. He wasn't sure what to do. And your mother begged him not to tell you, told him that if he ever loved her, he wouldn't. He said he needed to see you at least once, up close, or he might just go and tell you. Your mother could only agree, yet she would do it only if your father promised never to say anything, to stay out of your life.

Why would he agree to that? Magdalene asked, astonished, angry.

I cannot say. He told me he wondered what good he could do for you, Magda. You were already growing up with a father. He didn't even have a steady job at the time.

They were quiet. A lone bird whistled close to them. A jet thundered overhead.

Some would say, I guess, that Boogaloo lived a sad, lonely life. I would say one filled with love and pride for you. I remember once on the phone he couldn't stop talking about your going to graduate school. He kept saying, *How incredible, how incredible! The daughter of a man who spent much of his life in a field, working in the dirt. How incredible!* And he always dreamed you might one day find out about him and go see him. He would never go back on his word. He was honorable in that way.

I will go . . . I'll take Isabel and we'll see him.

They both looked up the trail; they heard Isabel laughing.

Where is he now?

I haven't talked to him in some time, but not that long ago he told me he was living near St. Joe, he had run into Ernest by accident, and they had eaten a nice dinner. And don't worry, Ernest never knew Boogaloo was your father.

You know what? And this might sound funny . . .

Changó blinked his left eye several times, the patch on his right eye twitching a bit.

There was a time when I thought *you* were my father.

He jerked his head back, his eye wide open. Me? What made you think that?

I don't know, really. I guess I was trying to understand who I was, where I came from. I listened to Ernest talk of you and your life, and then you were always drinking, you and Evelyn splitting up . . . Well, for four months or so I had this deep, mushy, nervous feeling in my stomach that the reason my mother was angry at you, why she was always trying to keep me away from Ernest, was because you were my father. Eventually the nervousness went away, and I realized I liked the idea that you were my father.

Magda, thank you.

One day I finally asked my mother if you were my father. She slapped me so hard across the face my ears rang with pain. She told me to never ask such a stupid question, and then she laughed and laughed in a way I've never seen her do, shaking her head. I knew she thought I was a little crazy, and I knew then you weren't my father.

Mamí, hurry up, Isabel yelled. A spoon banged against a pot three hard times.

Maybe we should go before they send the marines down here to get us, Changó said.

They turned toward the trail. Magdalene told him, Thanks, thanks for talking to me, and for bringing me down to this wonderful place.

He nodded, and then said: There's going to be a lot of good food.

I'm hungry.

Me, too.

Maybe you can lead the way up, Magda? I think it's too dark for me. Changó had his shoes in his right hand, the machete in his left. She slipped on her sandals.

Segudo.

She stepped forward. Changó handed her the machete, took her hand. They began the climb up the trail.

On the road leading from Abuelo and Abuela's were candles and lanterns, a small pink glow of sunlight still remaining on the tops of the mountains, the red road amber in the light. They were all walking together—Lillo, Abuelo and Abuela, Evelyn and Changó, Isabel and Magdalene—up the road to the festival. Magdalene carried a plate of pasteles, and walking beside her, in her white T-shirt emblazoned with the Taino image was Isabel, carrying a watercooler. They passed people who waved, called out Abuelo and Abuela's names. In the fields there were bonfires, the sky deep blue, darkening. She heard conga drums, a guitar, a soft voice of sorrow, and then clapping.

In the front yard of a coral-colored house a pig slowly turned over a long trench of orange and yellow and blue coals, its skin shiny and red and, in places, Magdalene saw the skin as almost transparent in its crispness, each turn of the pig setting in motion the illusion that when the pig was upright, for the briefest of moments, it jumped over the fire, its legs tucked under just as it leapt. Magdalene laid the plate of pasteles on the long table filled with food: pots of red and black beans; a huge bowl of white rice; a skillet of arroz con gandules; a pan of grilled chickens; a boat of tinfoil filled with braised beef ribs; a long, deep platter with bacalao in olive oil with onions and chunks of yuca; and a tureen of goat stew Abuela had prepared earlier and now set on the table, removing its cheesecloth cover in one quick pull. Abuela took the watercooler from Isabel and placed it on the end of the table. She broke off a chicken leg, wrapped the end of it in a napkin, and handed it to Isabel.

Evelyn asked, Magdalene, you hungry?

I feel starved for some reason.

Evelyn passed her a plate. Magdalene went straight for the ribs, and over a mound of white rice she ladled some goat stew, sprinkling hot sauce from an old rum bottle over the top. Biting into the beef she realized how tired she was; it had been a long day, a long past few months. The meat was garlicky, the tangy flavor of red wine vinegar subtle yet clear. The goat stew and rice was silky, the meat pungent, the sauce deeply laced with cinnamon and oregano. The sauce she sprinkled on top from the bottle had little pieces of Scotch Bonnet peppers in it, which now fired all the flavors in her mouth. Her eyes watered, her nose ran. The walk up the trail with Changó still burned in her calves, and she hadn't been able to shake the cool air from down below off her shoulders. She shivered uncontrollably. She took another bite of the stew, set her plate down. Hugged herself. She blew her nose in a napkin. Looking at Isabel standing next to Changó, Isabel biting into her chicken leg, her cheeks stained with grease and little black bits from the grilling, Magdalene wondered how she could even begin to look for her father, where would she find Boogaloo? How could she explain everything to Ernest, and then ask for his help?

Magdalene bent down, a napkin in her hand.

Come here, you, she said to Isabel, who stepped forward then lurched into Magdalene, her arms wrapped around her neck. She gave Magdalene a big, wet, greasy kiss on the cheek; Magdalene pulled her tight, held her. She then wiped her face, Isabel squirming.

Be still, still, just for a second. She wiped one more time, let her go. Isabel ran away from the table, following the rest of the family, who were making their way into a gathering of people on the side of the house.

There was a group of musicians in a half circle. They had guitars; a güiro; a tall, fat pair of congas; and there must have been thirty or so people surrounding them. They paused before their next song, whispering to one another, pointing at the family. The singer, who held a pair of maracas in one hand, stepped forward with a small stool in his other hand. He placed it a few feet away from the musicians, dead center in their half circle. He called to Changó, asking if he might join them for a song.

Changó declined, No, no, waving his hand, as if he could push the singer's request away. Many voices called from the crowd, trying to pull Changó forward into the circle of song. He shook his head, waving his hands in the air. Then a chant rose up for the guaracha "The Dance of the Tired Ox." The crowd clapped, and Evelyn and Abuela gave Changó a small push into the circle; he spun around like bees had stung his behind, waving his arms faster, and the crowd clapped louder, laughing. He smiled, stepped back, his hands in the air, *Okay, okay*.

Changó walked over to the stool, lifted it over his head, and with a wide arc brought it to the ground just as he sat down. The guïro player scratched one, two, one-two-three, followed by the guitar strumming the melody, and then the maracas joined in, followed by the congas.

Isabel clapped her hands and danced a little two-step Magdalene had never seen her dance before. She moved all around, following the projection of Changó's voice, all the while moving closer to him. When she danced closer she stopped her clapping, her feet kicking up red dust. He opened his arms and she stepped into them, Changó continuing to sing. His voice was deep and clear, and the only thing that distracted from it was the thick white patch over his eye, bright in the lantern light, his hair swept back off his forehead, his lips opened wide as he hit a high note. His energy seemed unlimited to Magdalene; how, she wondered, with the painful memory of his life around him, within this song, his eye—how could he sing with such passion and grace and beauty? The song became lovelier and more powerful as the crowd joined in, singing the chorus perfectly, singing with great reverence for the pathos the ox lived in.

Changó let Isabel go, stood, lifted his voice from down in his belly, wailing the last words in a jazzy improvisation:

> I'm no longer the tired ox
> I'm no longer the tired ox
> my eyes clear of sorrow
> tomorrow the road home dry
> red and hard
> without tears
> for I'm no longer dancing the dance
> I'm no longer the tired ox

161

The conga player followed the measure and flight of Changó's voice, striking a slow, hoof-trotting beat, a soft shake of the maracas coming in between each step, the guitar entering into the mix with a slow, mournful strumming. The crowd erupted in applause, and then they shouted:

Changólito
Changólito
Que viva Changó
Changó lives
Changó lives

All the musicians rushed forward and clapped him on the back, offering him thanks. A guitar player yelled, ¡Cuchillo, cuchillo! ¡Tráme un cuchillo! A man stepped forward and pulled a knife from his belt, the blade short and shiny. The guitar player took it, and in one elegant swipe cut all the strings from his guitar.

¡Para Changó—que viva Changó! he yelled, raising his guitar in the air, the stings swinging with the crowd's applause, whistles rising in the air. The guitar player pulled one of the strings from his guitar, bowed, and then handed it to Changó. Abuelo and Lillo came over, Lillo chewing on a piece of pork, Abuelo eating a pastele out of its leaf. Changó had wrapped an end of string around each of his hands and held it in front of Abuelo, who said something quietly to him. They looked at each other, Changó nodded, and then, for a moment, Abuelo clasped Changó's shoulder.

Magdalene turned, looking for Isabel, then followed a burst of loud laughter. She saw Isabel squeezing between a forming crowd. Abuela moved toward the crowd, which was now pointing and laughing louder, Isabel just out of her reach.

Underneath a mango tree, inside the crowd, there was a young man lying on the ground. He had no shirt, no shoes—only a pair of black pants, his belt missing, his right back pocket turned inside out, the white lining torn and frayed.

Someone said, Que pobrecito, what a poor soul, he sold his shirt and shoes to buy himself a bottle of rum.

The laughter rose again, burning Magdalene's ears. She felt Isabel tug at the edge of her shorts, and then pull her hand.

Mamí, Ernest, Ernestito. And then louder, Is that Ernestito, Mamí?

Magdalene looked into Isabel's eyes, touching the top of her head, without a word to say. She looked up, briefly, feeling everyone listening to Isabel's words as she pointed.

No, no, Magdalene told her. But Isabel yelled again, Ernestito. Mamí, look—Ernest. Magdalene lifted her from the ground and held her close.

Last night Magdalene must have called out to Ernest in her dreams; when she awoke she found Isabel standing next to her bed, staring. Isabel had said, Mamí, Ernestito's not here. She held Isabel tightly, kissed the top of her head, saying over and over again, *I'm sorry, I'm sorry, Isabel. You are right, oh so right. Ernest is not here.*

She briefly looked at the young man, his bare feet. She held Isabel tighter, then she let her down and took her hand. When she turned away she faced the family; they looked at her sadly. Then Changó came from behind them, almost running, screaming, *Ernestito, Ernestito,* tearing the patch from his eye. Evelyn tried to stop him but he broke past her. He walked over to the young man, calling for Ernest. He bent over and shook him.

Ernest. Wake up, Ernestito.

The young man jumped up, staggered for a moment, then fell to a knee. He looked at the crowd, at Changó, and then at the crowd again, his face filling with disbelief.

The crowd yelled, *Ay, Choló.*

His disbelief disappeared. He asked, What the hell do you want, Changó?

Changó turned away from him, his patch fluttering to the ground, his right eye patterned with deep red veins, his face wet with tears. He was suddenly somewhere else, his eyes seeming distant and blank to Magdalene, and he did not seem to feel the guitar string he had wound tightly around his wrist, his other hand pulling on the string, drops of blood beginning to fall to the ground.

No, Changó, it's okay, Magdalene said loudly.

She held Isabel's hand tighter and turned to Evelyn. She took Evelyn's hand, and she, Isabel, and Evelyn went to Changó. She felt Lillo, Abuelo, and Abuela following behind. She said to him:

Don't cry. Don't cry, Changó. Tomorrow, Changó, the next day, some time soon, Isabel and I will go home to Ernest, and we will tell him of you, we will tell him we heard his father singing.

Changó bit his lower lip, shook his head.

Magdalene let go of Evelyn's hand. Take my hand, Changó, Magdalene said. Take my hand and think of him; soon you'll take his.

She took the guitar string from his hand, slowly unwound it from his wrist, and then took Changó's trembling hand; trembling, she felt, with memories and love, and trembling, she knew, with the sorrow and the blood that ran into her hand.

There was a small curved inlet where the sea came in with big white rollers, and a single almond tree growing in a thick patch of grass, the tree seeming alone but never so—part sand, part grass, always of the sea. The smell of the almonds floating in the sea, Abuela had said, makes this a good place to say good-bye, so Lillo and Abuela raised the four bamboo poles and the wide piece of sailcloth they had brought, so they'd have greater shade next to the tree. They had set up a wooden table and some folding canvas chairs in the shade, and Magdalene could see her mother rubbing some lotion on Isabel's face, Abuela and Evelyn looking on, each with a yellow beach towel in her hand. The men—Lillo, Abuelo, and Changó—gathered around a small makeshift table of fruit crates, showing her stepfather how to play dominoes. She heard the dominoes crack on the table, followed by Changó's loud laughter, and then she turned away and walked toward the pile of black rocks shimmering with sea spray, the square bundle of envelopes tightly held against her chest.

She sat down on a flat and dry rock, a high rock so she could see out onto the sea, take in this last afternoon, the sun warm on her arms and legs, her face, the sea breeze blowing the ends of her hair back past her ears. She watched Isabel running along the beach with a blue bucket and shovel, little orange floats on her arms, Ramóna just behind her, looking lovely in her long red cotton skirt and white peasant blouse. Her mother and Isabel had been inseparable these past few days. Two nights ago, when her mother and stepfather arrived near dusk, bats swarming around the guava-colored top of the carro público that had brought them from the airport to Abuela's, Magdalene was shocked and unprepared. But then, when her mother finally saw Magdalene and Isabel standing on the front porch, she dropped her bag and ran from the road with her arms wide open, crying. Magdalene stepped down from the porch, and she, too, was about to run as she heard Isabel yelling, *Grandma, Grandma, Abuelita*. They held each other tightly, Ramóna, Magdalene, and Isabel, and her mother continued to cry, *Ay, mis hermosas, ay, my beauties, I'm sorry, I'm sorry, I'm so sorry*. Magdalene thought she was angry at her mother but could not stop crying herself, and in that moment of dusk, shivering with a cold and fever, Magdalene made no decisions, did not arrive at any conclusions—she simply felt a tug at her heart, and within her mother's fierce embrace she felt the flesh of a woman who didn't know her own mother that well, who left Puerto Rico long ago to make a place for herself in the world, and the only way she could do so was by believing—no matter how wrong or mean—that she was the only one who could control what was necessary to make that place.

Magdalene took a kleenex from her pocket, the square bundle lying on her thigh, and wiped the thick sweat from her forehead, the salt spray hitting her arms in tiny drops of blue and silver that felt welcomed by her fever. And as she had held her mother two nights ago, let her go, looked into her face, and then smiled as Isabel gave Ramóna a big kiss on the cheek, she knew it was unfair ever to say she hated her mother: she saw herself in the library writing away at a final paper; standing in the middle of her students, their desks in a circle, bent over colored papers and images, carefully cutting and gluing together the pieces of their lives; and then further back she saw that August when she left for college, and her mother held her tightly and told her how proud she was, how strong and smart and beautiful Magdalene had become. She had given Magdalene an expensive silver pen to take with her, and then she opened a small box that held two tortoise-shell combs resting on a nest of cotton. These have been in my family a long time, Magda, Ramóna had said. My mother gave them to me, and they went back in time to her abuela, a woman who was known to survive through anything, and who they say had these combs made from the shells of turtles she would catch from her own boat, shells she sold all over the Caribbean, even as far as the Yucatán. They had been standing on the Bond Street hill, Magdalene remembered, just before dark, looking down on the river filled with the last of the day's blue light. I wore them once when I was young, Ramóna said, but then never again—I never thought I was good enough or strong enough to wear them. But you are, mija, and you are leaving to go and become even stronger.

Magdalene blew her nose. She realized she had never worn the combs herself, she never felt worthy of them and had simply put them away. She knew then that when she arrived back to the mainland she needed to find her shell, El Guaracha del Mundo, and the tortoise-shell combs—they were somewhere in her old room.

She lifted the bundle from her lap and slipped a small folding knife out from the pocket of her shorts. She opened it, and in one quick pull cut the white string away from the banana leaf, the sea suddenly alive with timbre and bass, a lovely strumming from a guitar without strings. She looked to the sea, and far into the distance she saw a bank of silver clouds that seemed to cut the blue sky in half, and then as she followed the light of those silver clouds down to the sea, the water became black and almost flat. The sea's surface shook, and she could see silver curtains of rain falling from the clouds. She wiped the sweat from her forehead again and thought of how cold the sea must be out there, how cold and wet the sea became with that silver rain, and how loud the guitar played out there. She heard a dog yapping on the beach, and when she turned to its high voice there was a balding dog running down the beach, its bits of white fur matted and mottled with pink, chasing a little boy running with a long, flat stick, the boy striking a rusty bicycle wheel with the stick, his chest and arms gleaming with sweat and sun. They passed by, the boy lifting the wheel as he ran past the rocks, the dog still yapping and splashing through the waves. They ran more quickly toward a pier that stretched out into the sea, and out beyond the pier there was a small, lime green boat slicing through the sea, a puff of dark smoke rising from it.

She squeezed the bundle, let its shape form her hands. The white string fell against her legs, the corners of the banana leaf curling up, Magdalene smelling the rain, dirt, and plantains of these past months. The work and life. The deep song of memory. That night when her mother and step-father arrived, they threw together a quick dinner of salad, some fresh rice, and warmed leftover goat stew. They ate, and there was no room for anger because Isabel was so happy sitting next to Ramóna, talking a mile a minute about the things she had done and seen, and she tried to tell them all some broken story about a stream, a stone, and the sea. Everyone laughed and clapped, and Abuela then told some stories of Magda's abuela, Ramóna's mother. But then it became very quiet, and Magdalene's stepfather cleared his throat and spoke.

Ramóna, it is time to tell Magdalene.

Abuela said, We should leave you and your family alone, Magda.

No, no, I want my whole family here, and she called Isabel to sit in her lap. Once Isabel sat down, Magdalene said, I know Boogaloo—Manuel Perez—is my father.

Good, good, her mother said, crying, and then: I have no right to ask, but I'm sorry, so sorry Magda, and my only hope is that you'll forgive when the time is right.

The kitchen became quiet again yet filled with so much noise—the coquis singing in the night, leaves scratching against the tin roof, and then the thudding sound of a breadfruit striking the ground. A dog howled far in the distance, and when it quieted they could all hear the lone voice of someone singing out in the fields.

But it's all too late, Ramóna said, much too late. I'm so sorry, Magda, but Manuel . . . your father, Magdalene, Boogaloo, has died.

Magdalene held Isabel tighter, kissing her on the side of the neck, and she started to cry because that unknown place of hollowness she had carried around inside for so long was filling quickly—she saw it in their faces, Changó covering his eyes with his hands, Evelyn turning her head down and putting her arm around Changó; the tears streaming down Abuela's face as she and Abuelo stood and walked slowly out of the kitchen into the dark back field; the red cheeks of embarrassment and sadness on her stepfather's face; and the anguish of her mother's dark eyes searching for something to say.

How? she asked.

A stroke, Magdalene, her stepfather said. An aneurism. It was Ernest who came to see us; he told us.

There were immaculate cream-colored envelopes inside the banana leaf, the cotton paper soft to the touch; Magdalene approved of Ernest's lovely choice. Magdalene smoothed the front of the envelope out over and over again, rereading their handwritten names, *Isabel and Magdalene*. It had been a long day with her parents' arrival, and, sitting at the kitchen table, she realized Isabel had fallen asleep on her shoulder, and she stood and took her to bed. She laid her down and sat on the edge of the bed next to her. She could hear her mother and stepfather talking in the kitchen, and then crying. Magdalene cried, too. She opened the window to their room, let the moonlight fill her table, the floor, and felt so much hunger to see Ernest, to hold him in this moonlight, and to hear him share the story of her father's death. She needed Ernest more than she needed any anger or pain—she felt words and images returning to her, as if they were writing themselves within and naming that hollowed place, and she spoke them into the moonlight: *My father had the honor and dignity to keep his promise, and though he never spoke to me, I can hear him telling me I have to live with more than my memory.*

She turned the envelopes over, the flaps sealed in a blue wax, the wonderful raised image of festina lente: a dolphin and an anchor joined on the sea. The envelopes must have arrived in an envelope addressed to Changó; he had given her the photograph Ernest had included, with a small note inscribed on the back, and told her Ernest had wanted him to give her the envelopes. She thought Changó wanted her to read the note on the back, too, but when she placed the photograph on top of the envelopes, she realized he must have wanted her to see Ernest: standing outside a house, a wide smile on his tanned face, his hair wet and combed straight back, wearing a clean white sport shirt, with a splendid orange and red shawl wrapped around his neck, and just above his head a small alphabet of blue and white tiles on an old stone column, *Casa~Museo D Antonio Machado.* Just above each wax seal there was a faintly penciled number in Ernest's handwriting, and she broke the seal of envelope number one with the knife.

She couldn't bear to read them——for weeks they had lain unopened on the table in her room; she knew he would tell her once again that he loved her, and that they should be together. But she didn't want to hear it, was still afraid to become a part of his life, afraid she might get in the way of his becoming. When her mother arrived, she was the one to persuade her, to beg her to go back with strength if Magdalene's heart told her to be with him. Nothing can get in your way, she said. And now that she knew of her father's death, she recognized an odd presence: she heard her father asking her not to take part in the keeping of hurtful secrets. She pulled the sheet of paper from the envelope, unfolded it, and held it up in the sun for a moment, the blue of the sea entering into the cream-colored sheet, and she imagined that this was the beginning of the stories she and Ernest would share to complete their lives.

She could now see her mother sitting on the beach, her ankles in the sea, Isabel across from her as they played in the sand. Abuela and Evelyn stood waist deep in the sea, rubbing water on their arms and faces. Magdalene listened to Ernest.

Dear Isabel,

When I woke up this morning, I wondered if you might be seeing every morning what I saw once long ago.

Abuela stands in her open kitchen. Steam rises with the song she hums. She dances and sways to her song, moving back and forth from the table to the stove. Sunlight slants through the doorway, banana leaves shake in the breeze, shadows entering in waves behind sunlight and leaves. A hummingbird flutters above her shoulder, its purple throat turning silver within the color of Abuela's hair. She works between this morning's shadow and sun: she chops garlic, onions, cilantro, and tomatoes, and then adds them to a pan of simmering rice. You step forward, quietly, watch her pour achiote oil into the pan, the rice turning a deep yellow. Lightly she rubs the side of your cheek with the back of her hand, smiles, and then turns a small blue bowl over the pot, a stream of glistening gandules trembling into the pan. She spoons coffee into a boiling pot of water, then adds a small cup of cream and a couple of spoonfuls of sugar.

The kitchen: the doors wide open, windows without glass or screens, leaves and hummingbirds freely floating in, the sunlight filling the kitchen and tiger-striping the white-tiled floor. Such a lush silence: shaking leaves, fruits hitting the ground in a deep thud, Abuela's sandals scraping the floor, her spoon striking the side of a pot.

Mí amore, Isabel, sit down.

Abuela brings you a cup of coffee and a plate of yellow rice and gandules surrounded by slices of avocado. And when you bend over to smell—who knew garlic smells of yellow, peas can smell like limes, and onions are clear except for a hint of olive oil and salt—you close your eyes and feel you are becoming the steam.

Isabel, I write "Abuela," and I've been told this is wrong. I remembered her after many years of not seeing her, she lives so far away, and I almost forgot my time there—her flowered dress, her dark skin and silver hair, and how she was neither fat nor skinny but when she hugged me I felt she offered me every bit of who she was. What I've written here is the first time I remember my father's mother, and when I remembered the sound of her name, and I wrote "Abwela" in a small paper for school, the teacher called me to the side one day and said, You spell it, abuela, and without a capital. So I learned it, but I liked how she colored my memories, what she meant to me, so I also learned to make it my own, to spell it large the way it must be. Abuela.

Your great-grandmother, Isabel. I know you two must have splendid days together—sitting by the fountain in Rincon, walking on the red road in the twilight, watching the bats come out to welcome the night. Ask her to tell you the story of the stream in the mountain that runs all the way to the sea. I only hope to one day cook a meal for you and your mother like Abuela did on that morning.

Un abrazo
fuerte
de Ernest

That was enough. She needed not to open any of the other envelopes; it was clear to her that Ernest knew that Isabel was his daughter, that they shared so much Magdalene could not deny—and would never fully know. She quickly folded the sheet of paper, tucked it into the envelope, and pressed the seal hard. She bundled the envelopes back into the banana leaf and tied the string, thinking of how they could sit in Michigan some evening, and then she would listen to each envelope in the clarity of Ernest's words, his voice, Isabel at his side.

She closed the knife, slipped it back into her shorts.

The boat let out a deep, long whistle. Docked next to the pier, the boat billowed black smoke, idling. The engine died, and when the smoke disappeared, Magdalene saw the boy who had been chased by the little bald dog: now he ran across the sand toward the pier, his stick turning the rusty bicycle rim, the wheel spinning in the sand, the dog trying to catch it, a froth of waves knocking the wheel down, the dog jumping back with a yelp from the sea. The boy ran across the sand to the pier, then jumped down into the boat. Swiftly he reappeared, a fat burlap sack over his shoulders, his dark muscular legs struggling under the weight. He slowly carried the load down the pier—the men from the boat passing him quickly with two or three bags hoisted on their shoulders—and dropped the bag on a cart waiting at the end. He ran back to the boat, this time appearing with a long bundle of bananas.

Magdalene lifted her hands from her lap, holding them in the sun for a moment. They had become dark in these past few weeks, a deep chocolate color, and she remembered that Changó had said that Boogaloo recognized her because of how she held her hands at her side. She remembered that when he lifted the rum bottle out of the cooler, that summer day on Island Park, and walked away alone under the trees, her father's hands were long and graceful, beautiful and dark, except his right hand was missing half a pinkie. She had never remembered that about his hand, but then it came back to her that when Boogaloo had given her El Guaracha del Mundo, he placed the shell in one of her hands, and clasped her other hand briefly, and when he took his hand away she felt how smooth yet strong the nub of his finger was. Her hands had never known the work her father's had, how he may have looked at his missing finger every day and remembered his work, his memory of the fields. It was some accident, she thought, before my father was ever a cook. Maybe from a machete out in some unknown cane field.

Her mother and stepfather stood on the beach waving, Isabel in her mother's arms and between them. The rest of the family stood there, too, yelling for her and waving yellow towels. They all yelled for Magdalene to come back. Yesterday the house was so quiet, and Magdalene let her mother spend the day with Isabel, her stepfather going into town with his camera and notebook. That night at dinner the silence was too much, and Magdalene asked Changó, What was that song you sang the other night? He was chewing a forkful of yuca, his lips glistening with oil, and then he wiped his lips and took a long drink of cold water. He said it was an old, old story—and, he stressed, his closed fist lightly pounding on the table, it wasn't just his story, and it was repeated all the time in many different places. On the edge of a cane field that he and Boogaloo had worked in, they used to see an old white ox walking in the same circle. Chained to a mill, the ox had no choice but to keep walking, its deep path filling with spring rains, its belly wet with rain and sweat. We were little boys, he said, hugging himself, and our arms burned from unloading the carts of cane. He smiled and laughed, and started to eat again but put his fork down and said, That's where the song comes from.

And a great song it is, Changó's father added.

She waved back to her mother and stepfather, Isabel, the family. She stood up from the rocks, shielded her eyes from the sun, and looked out to the horizon. The boat whistled. She turned. The cart of goods started away from the pier, pulled by a team of oxen, the little bald dog yapping at the side of the teamster. The young boy stood next to the sea, the bicycle wheel against one leg, the stick against the other, drinking deeply from an orange soda, his arms and face glistening with sweat.

Boogaloo, Manuel Perez, my father . . . He had said my face was perfect. Always perfect.

She blew her nose again, pressing hard against the bones just below her eyes, hoping that her fever and cold wouldn't bother her when she and Isabel flew back to the mainland. Her mother yelled for her once again. Tonight, just before dark, she thought, she'd ask her mother to take her and Isabel to where she lived as a child, and as they walked toward that place, she would ask her mother to tell her how Ernest had come to see her and what he had said to make her come and find Magdalene and Isabel.

She waved again, smiled, and then stepped away from the rocks. Magdalene squeezed the bundle of envelopes to her heart, twice, stepped into the sea, and let the waves hit her ankles and knees as she walked toward the smell of almonds; her forehead no longer covered in fever; her hair blowing to the sound of each wave; the sea continuing on, caracole after caracole, slow, fast, slow—unfinished, eternal, touching regions far and wide, with and without names.

acknowledgments

The lines "The dream of one is the dream of everyone" (*el sueño de uno es el sueño de todos*) is a part of my memory and imagination—in translation—because of Rubén Blades' canción "Buscando América." Ernest Hemingway wrote in his novel *The Garden of Eden*, "All the yellow country and the white hills and the chaff blowing and the long line of poplars by the road."

Long ago I learned that mysterious and credible writing, that is, compelling writing, is never a solitary act. Given the communal tendencies of my writing, there are thanks in order to those individuals and institutions who collaborated on this novel.

Patricia Henley and Chuck Wachtel are the best teachers this young writer could have; they let me write, write, write, and their main concern, it seems, was to treat me with dignity, even if my language—my poor English—might not deserve it in the eyes of others. You both honored my heightened awareness of language's poetic possibilities. You continually read my work, offered me books to read, and then you guided me to return to a series of events to discover and invent even more in the moment-to-moment sensations of the fictional dream. I thank you both.

The Program for Writers at Warren Wilson College has been very important to me. It not only fostered my writing, it also helped me to develop my craft, articulate it, and acknowledge the poetic traditions that have helped me to make the most of my fiction writing. I thank the community of writers and teachers who make the program extraordinary. Special thanks to Andrea Barrett, Michael Martone, Pablo Medina, and Nahid Rachlin.

Devin and Paul, you've generously read and commented on my writing or helped me talk through some particulars—and at a time in my life, in a city, where aloneness was my fate. I now know that, as Seneca wrote, "only the most worthless of our possessions falls under the control of another. All that is best for a man lies beyond the power of other men, who can neither give it nor take it away." Our conversations stay with me.

I must thank the Indiana Arts Commission for the Individual Artist Grant that helped me to begin writing.

Patti Hartmann, acquisitions editor at the University of Arizona Press, I thank you for recognizing my writing, for working in my behalf with generosity, critical and imaginative insight, and for making publication a reality. For so long I thought this novel would never find a home, and now it feels like *I've* finally found a home.

about the author

Fred Arroyo is a writer of fiction, poetry, and essays. For the last six years he's taught writing and literature in the United States, and he taught a graduate seminar in Ethnic American Literature in Spain. Arroyo received graduate degrees (MA and MFA) in creative writing from Purdue University and from the Program for Writers at Warren Wilson College, and a PhD from the University of Wisconsin–Milwaukee. He is working on new fictions and completing a book of essays, *Close as Pages in a Book*, in which he explores his interest in literacy and the writing life, while returning to memories of childhood, migration, and work. Arroyo is an assistant professor of fiction writing at Drake University, Des Moines, Iowa. *The Region of Lost Names* is his first novel.